Blood of Pioneers

Divided Decade Trilogy
book two

Michelle Isenhoff

Edited by Amy Nemecek.
Cover design by Dale Pease of Walking Stick Books.
All rights reserved.

Lexile score: 780L

ISBN-13: 978-1499230536

Candle Star Press
www.michelleisenhoff.com

For Emily

Chapter One

Wayland, Michigan, 1862

One honest glimpse of freedom has the power to twist life into a coyote trap. Routines that once gave Hannah Wallace a measure of contentment now ensnared her, dulling her imagination, chaining her painfully in place. In contrast, her brother bounded down the street like a rabbit freed from a cage.

Hannah watched him with a mingling of jealousy and pride. He looked dashing in his Sunday best, buttons gleaming, hat set at a rakish angle, newly shined boots kicking up puffs of dust. He was young, handsome, confident, and off to save the Union. Oh, what she wouldn't give to be leaving town with him!

Seth had only been seventeen when fighting first broke out, not old enough to join up without lying like his friend Jamison Coops had done. Folks signed up in droves, afraid the war would end before they had a chance to make a name for themselves. Seth had begged and pleaded, cried and even swore, but Pa stood firm. War was dirt and illness and sweat and killing, and no underage boy of his was going to participate. Pa's pessimism didn't dampen Seth's enthusiasm any, but his sharp eye did keep him from sneaking off, so the boy had to wait.

Then early this summer the recruiters came back. Soon as Seth heard, he let out a whoop, dropped his pitchfork, and lit out for town. Hannah tagged along, positively green with envy, and watched him set his name down with a flourish. His lopsided grin sparkled with charm and innocence. "With a Wallace man in the mix," he boasted, "the war will be over in no time."

"That's the spirit!" the recruiter encouraged. After a year of fighting, volunteers had grown scarce. Returning veterans advertised the destruction of warfare too well. The dead spoke even louder. "I wish I had ten thousand more boys like you, son."

"Won't need 'em, sir." Seth swelled with pride and confidence. "I'll lick those Rebs myself. All the way back to Richmond."

Richmond! How Hannah would love to see it. Washington, too. And Charleston and Montgomery and the mountains and the ocean and all the other places the newspaper filled itself with nowadays. They sounded so far away—exotic and exciting. And her crummy brother would probably get to see them all.

She watched as Seth joined the gathering in the park square. A dozen recruits from the farms round about sat in the grass and on old stumps, rendezvousing for the first leg of their journey, the county seat in Allegan. Hannah knew many of them. Their number included a few older men, but most were young, raw-boned farmers leaving home for the first time.

Her eyes flicked immediately to Walter Beasley, whose wrists poked a good three inches beyond his cuffs. He had sprouted up faster than a new row of corn, and his poor mama never could keep up. But his smile was open and friendly, and Hannah had always liked him.

Next to Walter stood cocky little Tommy Stockdale, the blacksmith's son and her own brother-in-law, with his bellyful of wild stories and a penchant for thinking up ideas fool enough to land an entire Sunday school class in trouble. Her oldest sister, Maddy, had run off and married Tommy as soon as she turned sixteen. Mama and Pa didn't like the idea of her getting hitched so young, especially with a war on, but they figured stopping her would only push her into a peck of trouble, so they reluctantly agreed.

Walter slapped Seth on the back. "Glad you could join us, Wallace. Gunna need you for my rear guard. When they slap a uniform on this fine-tuned body, every girl from Wayland to Washington is going to come begging me to marry her."

"Sure," Seth jibed, "until you open your mouth and start talking."

Walter grinned.

"I'm sorry, gentlemen," Tommy informed them with mock dismay, "but the war will be over before we can even muster in. Someone leaked to the press that I was joining up, and the South entered into immediate peace negotiations."

The others moaned and rolled their eyes, and Tommy punched Seth on the arm good-naturedly. "What a time we're going to have, boys!" he whooped.

Hannah's attention was turned by someone calling her name. Wes Carver waved at her from across the street where he stood on a tree stump gawking at the new soldiers, plainly wishing he was among their number. His older brother had left several months before with a similar group of men. Since then his mother had discovered Wes drilling with a stolen kitchen broom more than once.

Hannah skipped over to join her schoolmate, passing between storefronts draped with red, white, and blue bunting. "Isn't this exciting?" she exclaimed.

"Sure! It's the only thing ever happens in this town. But don't tell my father I said so." He dropped his voice with a nervous peek behind him. "I'd catch it good if he knew I was here. According to him, all those fellows are off to certain death or dismemberment."

Hannah brushed off the dire prediction. "There wouldn't be any glory without a little risk."

Of course war had casualties. Every week or so the *Allegan Record* published a list of county men who had died or been injured in the various conflicts. Hannah had known some of them, but tragedy hadn't touched her personally. Death, for the greater part, remained distant and faceless. Stories of gallantry and bravery in battle, however, had grown in the telling until even a plucky girl could imagine herself a hero. Old men might complain of the war's cost and its length, but not Hannah.

"Danger just adds to the romance," she concluded.

"Romance!" Wes spluttered as if the word tasted of quinine. "You girls sure have a way of turning everything into ribbons and daisies. War is about honor! The South has challenged the North, and we have to fight them."

"Oh, blast your honor," Hannah scoffed. "This isn't a gentlemen's duel. You and I both know the South is just a bunch of dirty rebels who chose to disregard the law and leave the Union. I wish I could be the one to teach them a lesson."

Wes bit back a devilish grin. He never could resist a provocation. "Aw, you're just a girl."

Hannah stamped her foot with a crunch of gravel. "John Wesley Carver! I can shoot the eye out of a squirrel at a hundred paces!"

He crossed his arms. "That don't mean nothing. You couldn't shoot a person."

Hannah missed the mischief in his eye. "I could so!

They're nothing but stinking Rebs who need shooting, and if I can't do it, at least my brother can!" She could feel the heat rising in her cheeks and knew it wasn't from the sticky August weather.

Wes straightened, suddenly serious. "Is that your pa joining up with the boys?"

Hannah had seen him, too, and some of the color faded from the banners. "What's it look like?" she snapped.

"Thought he didn't hold with fighting any more than my pa."

"He don't."

"Then why's he in there? The fellows rankle him too much?"

Hannah didn't answer. Pa had taken some ribbing off a few of the neighbors. They said his son was a braver man than he, but Hannah knew that wasn't why he signed his name. The real reason was to keep an eye on Seth and make sure he didn't "get his fool head blown off." She had heard him say as much to Mama that very morning as they lingered alone at the breakfast table.

"The wheat should pay off the debt, Amelia," he had said. "Right now our son needs me more than this farm does."

"It's not the farm I'm worried about, Henry."

Hannah had chosen that moment to barge into the room, causing her father to slosh his coffee. "It's not fair!" she cried.

Mama sighed. "Not you, too, child." Her eyes were red.

"You and Seth both get to go off and do something important, but I'll be stuck on this farm for the rest of my life. I wish I was a boy!"

Pa wiped his hand with a handkerchief then turned to face her. His voice was as rich and brown as soil. "First of all, you're only thirteen years old. Too young for war even if

11

you were a boy. And second, you've just named two good reasons why you're needed here at home. With Seth and I both gone, your mama is going to need your help more than ever."

Hannah crossed her arms spitefully. "She's got Joel and Justin," she said, naming her older and younger brothers. "And Maddy's moving home, too. They can help her."

Pa stood and rested his hands on Hannah's shoulders. "It's noble of you to want to fight, honey, but the North is going to need a different kind of help from you. The Union will need what this farm can produce. How do you think the army gets its bread, its meat, its horses? You will be serving your country right here."

She had looked up at her father with tears brimming in her eyes, and it hadn't taken him long to discover the real reason for her outburst. "Aw, Peanut," he said, pulling her against him in a tight embrace. "I'll miss you, too. More than anything."

That made the tears overflow. "Don't go, Pa." It was one thing for Seth or Tommy to go seeking for adventure, but Pa? He belonged here with his family. Here with her.

Pa pulled her chin up and wiped her eyes with his sleeve. "I won't be gone forever, darling. I'll be home before you know it. And it will help me to know you're being brave."

She had promised. But now, watching her father join the others, her resolve felt as fragile as straw.

"Your pa should have stayed home." Wes frowned. "He's thirty-nine, for crying out loud. My brother says the old ones are the first to get sick."

Tears burned Hannah's eyes. "Shut up, Wes Carver! You don't know anything!" She punched him hard and flew across the fields toward home as her father took his first step down the long, long road to Allegan.

Chapter Two

Hannah dumped the pail of wood ashes into the barrel. A puff of fine gray powder rose up, filling the shed and making her cough. The morning lay thick and steamy, with a haze blurring the edges of the fields. It was the kind of morning that felt so much like the afternoon before that it was easy to forget there'd been any night to mark the passing. She slammed down the barrel lid and set the ashes to swirling. Then, wiping her hands on her trousers, she placed the pail inside the back door.

In the week since Seth had gone, she'd taken to choring in his clothes. Mama didn't like it much, but they were a sight easier to move around in than a skirt. And for some reason they made her feel closer to Pa, like the work she did in them was more important.

Hannah reached for the hoe just as her youngest brother tumbled from the house and grabbed it. "Mama said I have to work the garden today."

Hannah snatched it away. "Then who's going to feed the chickens and collect the eggs?" The garden had been her responsibility for three years now. She wasn't about to entrust her vegetables to an eight-year-old.

"Me," Justin sneered, jerking the hoe out of her hands. "And you won't hear me complaining like you always do, because I know what it takes to run this farm."

Hannah wrinkled her nose in disgust as she watched him march away. Since the men left, chores that had been as predictable as daybreak were being shuffled like a game of Old Maid.

"Don't you kill any of my plants, Justin Wallace!" she yelled.

He stuck his tongue out at her.

Hannah yanked open the door. On her left was the "gathering room," as Mama called it, where the family assembled around the fireplace at the end of every day. But even at rest hands were kept busy. A sewing basket and knitting needles always sat tucked away behind Mama's rocking chair. And the pile of wool that needed to be carded before it could be spun into yarn was a permanent fixture in the back corner. No matter how many hours Hannah sat brushing pieces of it between the two hand paddles, the pile never seemed to grow smaller.

The kitchen opened to the right. Hannah found her mother inside frying bacon and eggs that fragranced the whole house. The woman's face looked weary even though the day had just begun, but her spine was as straight as the pines growing along the river. Hannah wondered if she had a bout of the ague last night. The dreadful shakes were endemic this time of year, followed closely by fever. Everyone got it, but Mama suffered more than the rest of them.

"Did you send Justin into my garden?" Hannah accused.

The grease sizzled in the big cast iron griddle as Mama flipped an egg. "Yes. I need you to do the laundry."

"By myself?" she groaned.

"With Maddy. The hay is dry and Joel and I have to get it stacked before it rains."

"Maddy! Mama, I can't—"

"You can and you will."

"But Mama, you know how bossy Maddy gets. I'd rather hoe the garden."

"You'll be doing both if you don't stop arguing—with the memory of Old Hickory on your backside."

Hannah glanced at the wooden rod hanging behind the stove. Only twice had she needed an application. The smoothness of the grain was owed mostly to Seth's stubbornness, though Justin was doing his fair share to maintain the polish.

"While you're standing there, you may set the table."

As she worked, Joel came in with the milk and set it on the sideboard. Sandy-haired, patient, and shy, every girl in the red schoolhouse had a crush on him, especially Sue Ellen Huseby. Hannah made a face. Joel had never even met Old Hickory.

"Did you turn the cows loose?"

"Yes, Mama."

Mama set the eggs on the table with a clatter. "Very good. Go call your brother. Breakfast is ready."

The kitchen was Hannah's favorite room. Mama's pretty china decorated the corner shelf Pa had carved for her. The cook stove threw off a pleasant warmth, and the rich, smoky smell of bacon set her mouth to aching. As the family gathered around the table and bowed their heads for grace, Hannah thought to herself that any meal in this room was the best time of the day. It would have been perfect, except for two empty seats.

Hannah missed Seth and Pa. Life went on much the same, but the flavor was all wrong, like tea without enough honey. She missed her father's easy grace and the sense of security she felt when he was near. And she missed the fire and energy that made Seth so darn disagreeable but so much fun.

15

That same restless fire burned in her own veins, often blazing to life at the most inopportune moments. She wasn't like Joel, who could bury his feelings beneath a cool exterior. The apocalypse could happen in the backyard and Joel would go on milking the cows with hardly a lift of his eyebrows. No, Hannah favored Seth. Emotions flowed through her as powerfully as the waters of the mighty Kalamazoo River. And like Seth, her deepest, strongest current was a voracious appetite for adventure. A desire made so much worse by the boredom of everyday life.

Farm work was just plain dull. All the local adventures had dried up long ago, soon after her parents unpacked their wagon. At that time, Michigan was mostly just wilderness. Mama didn't much like to talk about those days, but Pa would. Hannah loved to sit before the fire of an evening and listen to him tell about their journey from Vermont to Michigan.

Soon after he and Mama were married, Pa got the itch to go West. So they packed up everything they could carry and floated down the Erie Canal on a line boat pulled by two mules. Then they boarded a steamship for Detroit. There they had purchased a team and a wagon and followed the old Indian trails to Allegan County. How Hannah wished they would have waited a few years so she could have shared in the adventure!

Back then, the farm was still a forest. Pa had purchased it with a mind to try farming. They had built a little log cabin where Seth and Maddy and Joel were born. Seth remembered hearing packs of wolves howling outside the cabin when he was little, and Pa had once shot a panther where the hen house now stood. One day a band of real Indians had walked through the farmyard, stopping to trade dried meat and colorful baskets for some of Pa's pipe tobacco and a length of woolen cloth.

But Hannah had missed it all. By the time she came

along, the family had already moved into the new frame farmhouse. Most of the wild animals had been killed or driven away, and the Indians who hadn't moved kept mostly to themselves. The county was getting downright civilized and it didn't suit Hannah one bit.

The old log cabin still sat on the edge of their farm, but it was only used for storage now. Hannah spent hours in it as a child, coercing Joel to play the part of her husband as they braved many dangers on the frontier, but it had all been make-believe. Every last real adventure had been used up, and Hannah had resigned herself to living with it.

Until war flared up in the East.

Now Hannah's head swam with new stories and ideas. Marching, camping, fighting, traveling to new places, maybe even seeing Mr. Lincoln himself! It sounded far more exciting than slopping the hogs, but once again she was doomed to miss it all.

"Isn't Maddy coming down?" Justin asked, cramming his mouth with one last bite of toast.

"She can smell breakfast," Hannah grouched. "Let her miss it if she chooses." Hannah was none too happy about sharing her room again.

"She isn't feeling well this morning. Let her be," Mama answered.

Mama always did have a blind spot for Maddy. Maybe it was because Maddy managed to keep her dresses unsoiled and her bows crisply tied. Or because she could make tiny, even stitches while Hannah's sampler looked like the cat sewed it. Perhaps it was because Maddy could make the shuttle on the loom fly nearly as fast as Mama.

Pa said it was because they were two peas in a pod. "Mama can remember acting and feeling just like your sister when she was a little girl. You're the one she can't understand, Peanut," he had said, swinging Hannah high in the air to make her squeal. "She just doesn't know what to do with a wild Indian child."

Whatever the reason, Hannah was content to shadow Pa.

Mama rose from the table and tied her hair up in an old handkerchief. She looked too fragile to work the fields. As if on signal, Joel pushed his plate back and headed for the barn.

"Hannah, wash the dishes then strain the milk and start the wash. Several shirts in my basket need mending. Also, there should be enough eggs to bring to town. Please put on a dress before you go. And tell Maddy to have lunch ready at noon.

"Justin, the girls will need wood split and brought inside. And fetch water for the washtub, too, please."

Still issuing orders, Mama went out the door with the boys, and Hannah set to work in the quiet house. First, she lined a sieve with cheesecloth and poured the milk through. Then she transferred it to shallow, scalded pans and brought them down to the cellar to let the cream rise. On her return, two buckets of water waited for her beside the stove. She set them on to boil and went in search of Maddy.

Her sister still lay in bed, the sheet pulled up to her nose.

"You've gotten lazy living in town." Hannah yanked at the covers none too gently. "Mama said you need to make lunch."

Maddy grabbed the sheet and rolled over. "Leave me alone. That's not for hours."

"Do you always sleep till eight o'clock? You missed breakfast."

"Thank goodness. I could hardly stomach the smell. Tell Mama to make corn mush tomorrow."

"Tell her yourself."

Hannah pulled off her trousers and considered her sister. Ever since she could remember, Maddy had tried to

18

manipulate the rest of them into doing things for her. And not just little things, either. Seth usually told her to stuff it, but once she had Joel cleaning the chicken coop in her place because chickens "gave her a rash." Justin, being youngest, was often pressed into service as well. But because they were both girls and were always being lumped together, Hannah had to endure more of Maddy than she felt was fair.

Hannah tugged an old dress over her head and struggled with the row of buttons. Then she saw a glimmer of opportunity. "Mama also said you need to help with the laundry, but if you're sick you can do the mending. There's a whole basketful downstairs." Hannah despised sewing.

Maddy moaned. "Did Mama make coffee?"

"You hate coffee."

"Is there any on the stove?" she asked, reaching for a wrap.

"Not anymore. I put wash water on."

"You didn't throw it out, did you?" It was more plea than question. Hannah shook her head.

Maddy relaxed. "Good. I'll do the mending. After I get some coffee. Will you bring me a cup?" she wheedled.

Hannah ignored her. "I'm off to the store."

"Wait!" Maddy rummaged in a tiny coin purse and pulled out a nickel. "Get me some soda crackers, will you?"

Chapter Three

Scorched, yellow grass scratched at Hannah's bare feet. Behind her, the sun had already burned off the morning haze, and wisps of hair that had wiggled free of her braids clung to the moisture on her face and neck. She should have finished the laundry first, before the heat became unbearable, but mornings always called to her. So she followed the parched wagon track two miles to town, dangling a basket of eggs from one arm.

Ahead, she could see a line of timber that marked the Plank Road where she would turn north. It was the finest road in the state, as far as she knew. Loads better than the muddy tracks that led everywhere else. Made of thickly sawn boards laid side by side, it stretched from Grand Rapids in the north to Kalamazoo way off south. Not much lay between the cities except woods and farms, but once the highway passed through, the little settlement of Wayland started growing like a newborn calf.

When Pa and Mama first settled, there was no town. Just the Lumberton mill three miles away, the old Indian mission away south, and here and there a farmer making a go of it between the stumps. In fact, as she padded up the planks, the first building she passed was Mr. Chambers' log cabin.

Nelson Chambers was the very first settler in Wayland. Of course, he had long since built a beautiful frame house next door. The old cabin was used as a school before the red schoolhouse was built, and for many years it housed church meetings when the preacher circled up this way. Now its thick, chinked logs stood as a monument to days gone by.

Just beyond Mr. Chamber's new home, where White Street crossed the Plank Road, stood the Wayland House. Mr. Chambers had built the hotel one year after the highway passed through, and now seven stagecoaches stopped there every day. Broad and two-storied, with a veranda stretching clear across the second floor, the hotel had a reputation for good food and hospitality. Travelers were always lounging on its shady porch or stretching their legs along the street in front of it.

Hannah spent a good deal of time there, too, when she could sneak away, because Wes Carver lived within its walls. His mother cooked for guests and kept the building spotless. Mr. Carver ran the front desk, figured paperwork, and acted as all-around handyman. Since the family had come to town, Hannah had visited often. Too often, her mother thought.

"Why can't you spend more time with girls your own age?" she had asked at dinner only a few weeks ago.

"Oh, Mama, the girls in this town are so dull!"

"You used to spend a lot of time with Mary Ann Harper."

Dear Mary Ann with her shelves of books and her boundless imagination. She had been a bright spot in Hannah's mundane world of chores. There in Mary Ann's room they would read and reread her collection of fairy tales. Or they'd act out their own dramas in faraway castles and peasant cottages. Sometimes they took their exploits straight from the pages of Mary Ann's beautifully illustrated volume of Bible stories, and Hannah would wonder why Sunday school couldn't be as much fun.

Mama used to say Mary Ann had a taming effect on Hannah. Playing with her was far different than following Seth on his rambles or climbing trees with Justin. But the adventures they dreamed up always felt real—until Mary Ann's father sold the farm and sent his family back East to stay with relatives while he accepted a commission in the army.

Hannah's father rescued her. "The Carvers are fine people, Amelia. Isaiah shows uncommon good sense, and Grace's cooking is known all along the stage route. I have no objection to our daughter's friendship."

It was a friendship Hannah had almost missed. The Carvers came to town soon after Mary Ann left it. In school, Wes had been assigned to the seat directly behind Hannah, and that first morning he had pulled her braid half a dozen times. By recess she was spitting fire. At her first opportunity, she socked him in the jaw and sent him sprawling into a mud puddle.

"Leave me alone, Wesley Carver!" she demanded, glaring down at him.

"I guess I will," he grinned, not at all abashed. He spread his hands apart in a helpless gesture. "If I promise not to tug your hair again, will you help me up?"

But when she grasped his hand, he pulled her down.

Thrashing in the mud beside him, with classmates looking on in varying degrees of amusement and horror, it suddenly struck her as terribly funny. She knew that, had the tables been turned, she would have done exactly the same thing to him.

They had both been sent home from school early that day. While they endured a scolding—dripping, disheveled, and nearly bursting with mirth—Hannah knew she'd discovered someone as spirited as herself. Someone amusing. Someone not afraid to have a little fun. They had called a truce before trundling home to their respective punishments and maintained a feisty friendship ever since.

"I have no argument against the Carvers, Henry," Hannah's mother continued. "But is a stage stop a proper place for a young girl to frequent, with all those strangers and their rough language?"

Hannah's father had reached across the table and grasped his wife's hand. He raised it to his lips and kissed it, eyes twinkling. "You worry too much, Amelia." That had been the end of it.

Now as she plodded into town, Hannah could see Wes waving from the hotel's open doorway. She waved back and watched as he turned away to answer his mother's call. She would stop in before trekking home.

Across the road from the hotel stood a crude little toll booth, so tight to the crossroads it nearly sat on them. It cost a penny to travel every mile of the plank highway, and Mr. Briggs perched inside with a fine view of vehicles approaching in both directions, waiting to collect payment. He knew all the stage drivers by name, and most of the other folk round about, and he was always the first to learn the latest news. That made him a great favorite with the town gossips, who paid him frequent visits on the presumption of collecting their mail.

Hannah ducked around the booth. To the east on White Street was Doctor Graves' medical practice and Mr. Burns' carpentry shop. She turned in the opposite direction, past a row of storefronts: Mr. Van Volkenburg's mercantile, Mr. Sadler's shoe store, Mr. Johnson's leather shop, and the forge operated by Tommy Stockdale's pa.

Before she covered half the street, a door opened and Mrs. Clark marched across the dusty road. The old woman took in boarders and operated a millinery out of her home.

"Hannah!" she snapped. "Your mother came in to see me this week. Tell her I've thought about it but I simply must have hard currency for the bonnet she wishes me to make."

Mrs. Clark always reminded Hannah of a turtle. Her overlarge head swiveled on a skinny neck, and she peered out from behind bifocals that magnified her eyes.

Hannah paused, frowning thoughtfully. "I'm not sure if that will be possible, Mrs. Clark. Coins are hard to come by. But we have plenty of pumpkins, potatoes, eggs…" She held up the basket.

The old woman snorted. "A pantry full of surplus farm products is exactly what I do not need. I have my own garden, thank you. I want legal tender. Times are tough, and there are plenty of folks who would take advantage of a lonely old woman."

Hannah's mouth tightened as she bit back a reply. Mrs. Clark's husband had died years ago, on their way to Michigan, and the widow had supported herself by teaching school before opening her shop. Hannah said a silent prayer of thanks for her new schoolteacher, Miss West.

"I'll tell her, Mrs. Clark."

"See that you do," the woman barked and closed herself back inside her house.

Hannah walked on. Through a gap in the storefronts she caught sight of the park square, looking scrubby and forlorn. Maybe someday the square would become be a beautiful common area suitable for a proper town. But apart from the handful of rough buildings lining the crossroads, Wayland was mostly undeveloped lots and sawn-off stumps, and so was the park.

Hannah turned into the very last store with a sign that read "Lawson's Dry Goods" in bold, blocky letters. The two-story building hadn't yet weathered to the dull gray of its companions. Timothy J. Lawson lived in the apartment above it, alone except for the company of a big orange tomcat named Horatio.

"Good morning, Hannah!" boomed the shopkeeper.

Mr. Lawson towered over most of the other men in town. He wore a full beard, and his apron looked ridiculously like a washrag stretched around a barrel, but not a soul dared tell him. He had tidy hands and gracious manners, and Hannah fancied he looked something like Goliath from Mary Ann's Bible story book, only friendlier.

"Good morning, Mr. Lawson. I've got some eggs from Mama." Horatio rubbed against her ankle, and she reached down to scratch under the cat's chin.

"Fine. I'll take them." He placed them carefully into a blue and white enamel bowl then opened the till. "I owe you seventeen cents," he said, counting the coins into her hand.

She handed a nickel back. "I need some soda crackers, please. For my sister."

As he scooped the crackers, he asked, "How's she doing? Poor kid, brand new husband gone off to war."

Hannah scowled. "Same as ever. Irritating as holey stockings."

Laughter rolled out of his chest like thunder echoing through a cavern. "I've always admired your spunk, Hannah." He dropped in several gumdrops before handing her the package.

She brightened. "Thank you, Mr. Lawson!"

He called out as she left, "Tell your ma the town council has called for a meeting in the schoolhouse on Thursday evening to discuss how the community might help families facing foreclosure."

"I will!"

Darting around a pair of horses hitched to the rail outside, she made a beeline for the Wayland House, but Mr. Briggs hailed her from the toll booth. "Hannah, come here!"

She changed course immediately.

25

Mr. Briggs was tall and spare. When he sat on his high stool watching for the stage, his legs tucked under his chin, he looked just like the daddy longlegs spiders that climbed the timbers of the barn. And he was never without his pocket watch, an heirloom from his grandfather. She often thought the fine gold chain dangling down his shirtfront would better befit a gentleman with a wider stomach to stretch across.

"Got a letter here from your pa."

Forgetting her manners, she snatched it away, tore open the envelope, and stared down hungrily at her father's cramped handwriting.

"Good news, I hope?" The postmaster looked on expectantly.

Hannah tucked the precious letter back into the envelope with reluctance. "Sorry, Mr. Briggs. I think it would be better to read this around the dinner table with my family."

"Of course you should," the man agreed, concealing his disappointment with a friendly pat on Hannah's shoulder. He was distracted by a wagon approaching the toll gate. He pulled out his watch and glanced at its face. "Eight forty-five. Mr. Lark's late getting to town this morning."

"Norton," the farmer called to Mr. Briggs, "you tell your boss this toothpick road is getting rickety as an old hen house. 'Bout broke an axle back near Watkins' swamp."

Hannah didn't wait to hear Mr. Briggs' response. She tucked the letter safely in her egg basket and crossed to the hotel.

She entered a spacious lobby with a stairway leading straight up to the guest rooms and a hallway that divided the building in half. Tucked in one corner, underneath the mounted skin of a huge bear Mr. Chambers had shot his first winter in Wayland, a Franklin stove stood ready to heat the room in cold weather. Mr. Carver sat behind an over-sized desk on the left side of the room, engrossed in his ledgers and books.

"Good morning," Hannah called cheerily. The man answered with a distracted wave.

A cozy parlor extended off the lobby, opposite the desk. Here travelers often lounged about, easily identified by their newspapers and carpetbags. The front windows gave them an excellent view of incoming stages.

Hannah entered the dining room situated in the hotel's left wing. On most evenings, the room filled with local farmers who propped muddy boots around the fieldstone fireplace and nursed pints of ale, but this morning only four guests sat eating breakfast.

Mrs. Carver emerged from the kitchen with a coffeepot in one hand and a plate of flapjacks in the other. "Hannah!" she exclaimed, pouring a refill. "You're in town bright and early. Are you running errands, or have you come to see Wesley?"

"Both." Hannah smiled. "Is Wes free?"

"He's hauling some firewood, but he'll be finished soon. Sit down and visit with me a moment."

Mrs. Carver was apple-faced, motherly, and as chatty as a squirrel—perfect for putting travelers at their ease. "Tell me, dear, how are things going with your men folk gone? I hear Mrs. Parker down Bradley way lost her farm. Her husband died at Fort Donelson, and she just couldn't make a go of it without him."

"We're doing fine, thank you, ma'am." Hannah sat on one of the straight-backed wooden chairs. "Joel says the harvest looks promising."

"Then let's pray the weather holds. But goodness! The dust does pour in thick through the windows this time of year!" She brushed at a gritty seat with a corner of her apron.

Paperwork set aside, Mr. Carver strolled into the room. He was short and round, with a balding head and a heavy

27

mustache. He poured a cup of coffee and rested a booted foot on the chair opposite Hannah. "Have you heard from your father?"

"I have a letter right here." She indicated her basket. "I'm saving it."

"Good girl." Setting his cup down, he swiped once at his forehead with the rag he used to clean tables. "Dang foolish war. You be sure and let me know if your family needs anything."

"Thank you, Mr. Carver. I will."

At that moment a lean, bandy-legged man sat down at the next table. Hannah couldn't have ventured a guess at his age, but his skin looked like leather pulled from the vats at the tannery north of town. A scraggily beard, mostly gray, brushed the top of his chest, and Hannah thought he looked exactly like a California forty-niner right out of the pages of her history book.

"Good morning, Mr. Covington." Mr. Carver nodded agreeably. "How was your first night in our fine little village?"

"Terrible." The stranger rubbed at one thin shoulder. "The ropes under my bed were so loose, whoever slept in it before me must have been a horse."

"Hmm, yes. I'm terribly sorry about that. I'll look into the matter directly."

"And the water in my room has turned brackish."

"It is rather difficult to keep anything fresh in this heat, but I'll see to it that your pitcher is refilled immediately."

Mr. Carver saw Hannah looking on. "Mr. Covington, may I introduce you to Miss Hannah Wallace? She lives on a farm just outside town. Hannah, Mr. Elijah P. Covington."

"Hello." Hannah smiled. The man didn't look up but grimaced and waved her away with a flick of his fingers.

"Mr. Covington is an artist from New York City who

plans to stay here with us for some time."

"Only until more suitable arrangements can be made," he grumbled in a voice as dry as road dust. "Can I get some breakfast? Or do I have to make it myself?"

Mrs. Carver called out cheerfully from a few tables away, "I've got hot flapjacks on the stove. Coffee?"

He gave one abrupt nod.

While she was gone, Hannah tried polite conversation. "You don't look as I fancied an artist would, Mr. Covington. But then I've never met one."

"Well, I've met plenty of impertinent girls in my day, and I've no use for another." But when his glance finally fell on her, he fixed her with a keen stare, narrowing his eyes as he studied her face. "On second thought, you just might do. A farmer's daughter, you say?"

Hannah didn't answer. She grew uncomfortable under his scrutiny.

"Yes, yes," the artist continued, standing to view her from another angle. He took in her braids, her bare feet, and her worn, patched dress. "A bit plain, skinny, freckled, but I could work around all that. Those eyes! They're just the shade of blue! Cadmium, I'd say. Yes, yes, I believe you're just what I'm looking for."

Mr. Carver cleared his throat meaningfully. "Hannah, why don't you run along in back and see if Wes is done with his chores yet."

But before she could move, Mr. Covington grabbed her chin and turned her face, studying it in the light from the windows. "Never mind, Carver. I plan to do a series of paintings while I'm here. Family farms, tranquil settings, the sort of rubbish folks idealize in time of war. I believe this girl might be just the subject I'm looking for. Think her father would grant permission?"

Irritated, Hannah slapped the man's hand away. "Mr. Covington," she asserted, "you are an arrogant, conceited

29

old man, and you smell like an ape. I would not help you if you got down on your knees and begged me!"

Chapter Four

Hannah stormed through the hotel's kitchen door and immediately regretted her words. News of her outburst was sure to get back to her mother, and that meant a guaranteed appointment with Old Hickory. But Mr. Covington deserved every insult. The way he had handled her—why, she steamed just thinking about it!

She was startled by the sound of wood dropping onto a pile. "Hey, Hannah, you're all red. You just been kissed?"

She whirled around. "Wes Carver, you're about to kiss my fist!"

"All right, all right! Sorry," he laughed, raising both hands. "Jiminy, what's got your dander up?"

"Oh, it's that Mr. Covington! He's a horrible old man!"

Wes rested one haunch on the side of the wood box. "He's a crotchety old thing, ain't he? Some folks turn lemons into lemonade, but he can turn cherries into pickle juice."

He peered into the egg basket. "Breakfast?" he asked, indicating the crackers.

"Of course not. They're for Maddy."

"Oh, I forgot the prodigal has returned. How is her royal highness?"

Hannah grimaced. "At least she's one more body who can pitch in and work."

"Busy?"

"I'm stealing time right now."

Wes grinned. "Then I'm flattered you'd risk your mama's wrath just to catch a glimpse of my handsome mug."

"You idiot," she chuckled. "I came by to see if you wanted to take Ol' Joe out next week."

"Sure. Can you sneak away?"

"I think so. And Mama couldn't argue if we came home with something for the pot."

They chose a day, and Hannah crept out the back door to avoid Mr. Covington. She was soon out of town and leaving the planks for the rutted wagon track that led home.

She passed the Burgess farm on her right. Mr. Burgess was a kindly old man who ran a small dairy. He had three grown sons who trotted off to war at the first bugle call. The youngest had promptly died at Bull Run, but that hadn't discouraged the other two from reenlisting when their terms were over. Mama sometimes called on Mrs. Burgess. She said it was her Christian duty.

Their nearest neighbor was Mrs. Patton. Her son, Peter, was good friends with Justin. Her husband had been deployed with the cavalry somewhere in Tennessee. Mr. Patton kept a herd of small, sturdy quarter horses that he worked diligently to improve. He was always trying to talk Pa into selling the north pasture, but Pa never would oblige. The herd was smaller now, with many of the animals sold to the army.

Hannah climbed the rise that overlooked her own farm. Golden wheat stretched in waves to the tree line beyond. She could see Mama and Joel forking hay into the wagon in the pasture. Justin was on top stomping it down as fast as it was thrown up to him. They had cut it last week and left it to dry in the sun. Now it was nearly all stacked in huge piles by the barn door.

The pumpkin field lay beside the barn, dotted with hundreds of swollen fruits already beginning to turn orange. Beyond them, the brown, wilted foliage of potato plants marked a wealth of food hidden just below the soil. She could see the milk cows grazing at the edge of the woods and a handful of chickens milling among them, pecking the ground. Several outbuildings ranged across the yard, and in their center, like a mother hen gathering her chicks, was the farmhouse.

As Hannah strode down the hill, she passed under the shade of a huge maple tree standing like a sentinel above the farm. Mama came here a lot, but Hannah hadn't visited since last year. She stopped now, her eyes coming to rest on the small wooden cross pounded into the ground and carved with the name Jeremy Tyler Wallace.

Hannah's earliest memory was of the day her brother was born. She didn't remember his birth, really, just his passing. Though she wasn't quite three at the time, she could still see Pa sobbing into the tiny bundle of cloth. It had frightened her.

She had tried to bring back her old Pa, the one who laughed and played with her. She had placed her arms around his neck and kissed his wet cheeks, but for the first time in her life her childish caress had no effect. And for the next several days, her beloved Pa was lost in a world she could not penetrate.

Hannah couldn't comprehend his grief. Her young mind understood only that the baby had been mighty important to Pa, that he must have wanted that little boy even more than he wanted her. She was older now, but it was a thought that never quite left her.

Maddy was sitting in Mama's rocking chair sewing on

a loose button. An empty coffee cup sat beside her on the floor. She didn't look so high and mighty today. In fact, she looked as rumpled as a fox-chewed hen. Hannah tossed the parcel of crackers into her lap and scampered upstairs to don her trousers.

Out in the yard, the huge metal washtub waited for her. She filled it with steaming water, added clothes and lye soap, and stirred the mixture with a wooden paddle. It was hard work dipping, scrubbing, rinsing, and wringing alone, but her ears were free of Maddy's nagging and her fingers were free of the mending needle. In just a few hours, the laundry hung in rows straight enough to please any disciplined regiment.

Mama and the boys came in from the fields at noon, sweaty, tired, and itchy with chaff. Hannah cared for the big work horses while Joel drew water from the well to wash. She could hardly wait to surprise them with Pa's letter. They clattered into the kitchen, drawn by the thick smell of cooking food.

Maddy had made biscuits and fried up thick slices of ham. The table was loaded with fresh green beans, fat tomato slices, cabbage slaw, and giant lettuce leaves rolled up with vinegar and sugar. Hannah's stomach rumbled louder than a dray cart on the Plank Road, and she could hardly let up drooling over the fixings long enough to bow for the blessing.

For several minutes, there was only the sound of chewing. Then Justin piped up, "Maddy, you don't cook half as bad as Tommy said."

That earned him half a biscuit flung in his direction, but it started the family talking.

"I saw Mrs. Carver in town this morning," Hannah volunteered. "She sent her greetings."

Mama looked up with interest. "Is she well?"

"Seemed so."

"Has she heard from Marcus?"

Hannah had forgotten to ask, even though Wes's older brother was a great favorite of hers with his quick wit and good-natured teasing. He'd been wounded recently at the Second Battle of Bull Run. "She didn't say."

"Me, Joel, and Mama got two loads of hay hauled," Justin stated proudly, "while you were jabbering in town."

Hannah pulled a face at him when Mama wasn't watching. "Bet they weren't as big as Pa's loads."

Mama shot her a warning look. "Hannah, the potatoes need digging this afternoon. Hitch up Rounder to the small cart after lunch and you kids get a start on it. Maddy can help Joel and me finish the last of the hay."

Joel spoke up. "I went around to Yancy's yesterday evening. He's coming this way with his thresher at the end of next week. If we're going to be ready for him, we need to start cutting and shocking the wheat tomorrow."

"Fine," Mama agreed.

"I could sure use a strong team of hands for the harvest," he continued, "but there just aren't enough men around."

"I can help!" Justin piped up.

"We'll all help," Mama said with a look around at the girls.

Maddy and Hannah both groaned.

Joel looked apologetic. "We'll need everyone. If we can cut it and get the use of that machine, I think we can pay off the bank with plenty to spare."

The last five years had been tough everywhere. Thousands of banks and businesses had failed. Hannah hadn't really understood when Pa explained that the depression was caused by a war between faraway England and Russia. She just knew the wheat her father worked so hard to grow sold for such low prices he could barely cover the expense of growing it. Twice he had to borrow money. But this year,

35

because of the war at home, prices had risen dramatically.

"That reminds me," Hannah said. "Mr. Lawson told me there's a meeting on Thursday about all the foreclosures."

"Did he say what's being suggested?" Mama inquired.

"No, just that the community wants to pull together to help."

"Tommy's pa says Lawson's a crook and a cheat," Maddy said, tossing her hair.

Hannah snorted. "Mr. Stockdale also thought he saw Jefferson Davis in the Wayland House last week. He's just sore that Mr. Lawson beat him to those forty acres Mr. Brewster was selling."

"He snatched them up right quick," Maddy pointed out, "and he bought the Nash place."

"So what? They're next door to each other."

"How'd he get the money, smarty?"

"Maybe he sold a farm back East like everybody else." Hannah had no patience for her sister's or Mr. Stockdale's suspicions.

"Tell me, what does he need all that land for when he runs a store?"

"Maybe he plans to farm it," Mama suggested mildly.

"He hasn't done it yet, and he's been here eight months."

"And in that time he's taken a leadership role it the community, become a deacon in the church, and he treats people with respect and fairness. I won't hear ill spoken of him in this house." Mama put an end to the subject. "Joel, you and I are going to attend that meeting. As soon as we pay off our own debt, we'll be in a position to help others."

Joel grinned. "We'll have enough left over for shoes."

"And candy!" Justin piped up. "And I want a jack-knife!"

"I'll buy a length of that new lace in Mr. Van Volkenburg's store," Maddy added.

Mama smiled and ten years melted from her face. "How about you, daughter?" she asked Hannah. "What would you like?"

Hannah glanced at the empty chair and shook her head. "I just want Pa home."

The joy in the room deflated like a spent bellows, and Justin glared at her accusingly. In the silence Hannah pulled the letter from her pocket. "I stopped by the post office."

Chairs scraped backwards and three bodies lunged at her, grasping for the precious envelope. Hannah jerked it away and handed it to her mother. Mama fingered the torn flap questioningly.

"I didn't read it. I almost did, but Mr. Briggs was standing there waiting to hear."

Mama pulled out the letter and drew a shaky breath.

August 18, 1862

Dear Amelia, Madeline, Joel, Hannah, and Justin,

It does me wonders just to name all of you. I miss you terribly. Soldiering is a completely different world for a lifelong farmer, and I confess I haven't taken to it easily. But Seth thrives on the routine, the discipline, and the drilling. He is all energy and enthusiasm and already a great favorite with the men.

We have officially mustered into the 17th Michigan Infantry, company D. We picked up several fellows on our way to Allegan. Do you remember Eli Wallington out Hopkins way? His son Wilber joined, along with a few fellows from Dorr. In all, there's thirty-two of us from home. Tommy has kept us in stitches with his stories and antics, and Walter eggs him on.

We caught a train in Kalamazoo. It's a marvelous fast way to travel, smooth as a duck on water, though I suspect the accommodations might be better for civilians. We arrived in Detroit overnight. Then it didn't take much to pass the physical. "Lift up one leg, then the other. Throw up one arm, now the next. You're healthy. Here's your uniform." A few fellows tried to fail the exam. I suspect a good many others joined up just to beat the draft that Lincoln will certainly enact.

I dearly miss your cooking, Amelia. I'm getting heartily sick of beans and boiled potatoes, though I know there may come a day when I remember them with fondness, so I try to keep my complaints to myself. Most of the fellows shore up well, too, though we have a few grumblers, especially after guard duty in the rain. But mostwise the boys make the best of things, and there's plenty of jokes and songs and music. But even at its best, barracks life cannot compete with home.

I love you all.

Most affectionately,
Henry Stanton Wallace

Chapter Five

Hannah plunged the iron fork into the ground, leaned her weight against it, and popped up a handful of potatoes. She carefully placed them in the cart. Behind her she could hear Justin working in the next row, grunting each time he speared the soil. Between them, waiting patiently, stood Rounder. Occasionally the white horse would shake his head at the hovering black flies and his harness would jingle, or he'd paw a furrow in the dirt, gently chiding the slow children.

More than any other object on the farm—except, perhaps, for the empty kitchen chair—Rounder reminded Hannah of her father. He was Pa's horse, a Morgan Pa had raised from a colt, and there wasn't a finer saddle mount in the county. Beautiful, with a proud head and expressive eyes, the gelding was gentle, dependable, and so intelligent he often knew what was required of him before he was asked.

Hannah remembered riding double through the woods with Pa when she was only five or six years old. There had been a windstorm the day before, and Pa was checking for new deadfall and marking damaged trees to cut for firewood. Rounder had been picking his way down a trail they often used when he turned off for no apparent reason.

"Hi there, Rounder," Pa said, turning him back. "It isn't time to go home yet."

Unexplainably, the horse turned in the opposite direction. Pa set him straight again, but after a third time, Pa stopped and searched carefully in all directions.

"What's wrong, Pa? Why won't he go?"

Pa sounded apprehensive. "I don't know yet, Peanut, but if Rounder doesn't want to go down this path, neither do I."

Hannah remembered scanning the woods with delicious shivers tickling her spine. She wasn't really afraid with Pa sitting behind her, but she half expected a bear to come pouncing out of the shadows.

Suddenly a crack like a rifle shot startled her out of the saddle, and a tree as thick around as Rounder's chest toppled across the path ahead of them. It groaned as it fell, smashing the underbrush around it.

Pa sucked in his breath. "I reckon you earned your oats today, boy," he praised, patting the horse's neck. He nudged Rounder forward, and the horse went willingly, stepping lightly around the quivering branches.

Thud, thud, thud. A handful of Justin's potatoes tumbled off the cart and plopped in the dirt. He scooped them up impatiently and tossed them back on the pile.

"Be careful, you big oaf! They'll spoil quicker if they bruise." Hannah grabbed up the reins to drive the full cart to the cellar. "That's exactly why I told Mama not to let you into my garden," she muttered. "You don't know how to handle anything carefully."

Justin made a face. "Gardening is for women. I'd rather do a man's work, like stacking hay." He looked longingly to where Joel worked in the distance.

"Mama's doing that just fine without you, and she's no

man. Neither is Maddy. Neither, in fact, are you."

He raised a stubborn chin. "I will be someday, but you'll still just be a dumb girl, no matter how much you wear those silly trousers."

Hannah turned scarlet with anger. "One woman is worth ten men. Without women, men would go extinct."

"Without women always telling them what to do, men coulda conquered the whole continent by now, all the way to the Pacific Ocean."

She gave him a look of pure disgust. "Lewis and Clark wouldn't have even found the Pacific without Sacagawea. Face it, Justin, women can do anything men can do, only better."

He snorted with contempt. "Except vote."

Hannah gave him a shove that landed him in the potato patch. "Perhaps if you were a man, which you aren't, I would let you drive Rounder to the house. But he's far too valuable to entrust to a little boy."

While he still sat on the ground, Hannah flicked Rounder hard, jouncing the cart over the rough ground, no longer caring if the potatoes spoiled. She had a third of the tubers stashed in the cellar before her brother even stalked into the yard. She worked beside him in tight-lipped silence, wondering if he noticed that she filled three boxes to his two. No boy—not Joel, not Justin, not even Jeremy, had he lived—could have worked faster.

***

A few days later, Mama and Joel prepared for the foreclosure meeting after supper.

"May I go with you, Mama? Please?" Hannah begged, swiping at a plate with a damp towel. A drive to town sounded more entertaining than staying in the house with Justin all evening. Maybe she'd even find Wes.

Maddy handed her another plate and butted in. "Have you finished churning the butter?"

"Yes."

"What about those socks that need darning? Winter's coming."

Hannah scowled. "You're not my boss."

"And the peppers you picked this afternoon," Maddy continued, "need to be cut up and hung over the stove to dry."

"Oh, Mama," Hannah pleaded, turning to her mother, "can't I do that in the morning?"

Mama overheard the whole exchange. Her face softened. "I suppose you can. Get your shawl. The air feels damp."

Hannah squealed and ran to fetch her covering.

Joel already had Rounder hitched to the small cart. He handed his mother into the seat while Hannah jumped in back, sweeping aside dirt and tossing out a severed potato. Then Joel climbed up beside Mama and took the lines. Somehow in the last few weeks he had quietly stepped into Pa's shoes.

A light slap and the cart bumped over the wagon track. The ruts were only slightly sticky from a shower the day before. At the Plank Road, Hannah laid her head against the cart's rough bottom to feel the vibration in her ears. She could almost imagine it was the sound of cavalry thundering across distant hills. With her eyes closed, she was one of them, driving toward battle, horses stretched out low, pistols drawn, sabers gleaming. She could feel the wind on her cheeks, hear the throb of artillery, the frenzied shouts of men, the clash of steel on steel...

The cart jolted into the schoolyard and stopped next to several other wagons. The schoolhouse sat a little apart from town, flaming red in the failing sunlight. Hannah scampered past it in the direction of the Wayland House, but her mother called her back. "I won't have my daughter prowling about town at night. Stay in the schoolyard."

Hannah kicked a tree swing dangling above a patch of gray dirt. "Aw, Mama!"

So much for finding Wes.

Settling on the sawn board, she nudged herself back and forth and watched the townsfolk file into the clapboard building. Sue Ellen Huseby arrived in a wagon with her parents. Two years older than Hannah, the girl pulled the highest grades in school and played the only piano ever lugged into town, and her singing voice could transform the Sunday schoolhouse into a cathedral.

Hannah found her exceedingly dull.

"Good evening, Hannah." Sue Ellen smiled, detouring toward the swing. "Is your family here?"

Hannah jerked her head at the building. "Joel's in there."

The older girl's cheeks pinked. "I didn't mean—"

Hannah shrugged. "What's in the bag?"

"My knitting," Sue Ellen answered, holding it up. "I thought I'd stay busy while I listen."

"You're going in there?"

"Of course. Aren't you?"

"Are you kidding? I've wasted too much of my life in that room already." *Let Joel and Mama figure it out.* She'd stay outside where it was cool. "I think I'll see how high I can climb in this oak tree before I get stuck."

Sue Ellen gave her a quizzical smile as Hannah shimmied up the swing rope and threw a leg over the lowest branch. "All right, then. I'll see you later."

Hannah was already halfway up the tree and happy to watch the girl leave. It wasn't that Sue Ellen was snobbish or unkind. She was pleasant, she had no vices, and everything she began she finished well. But she was all industry and no imagination. The girl was boring, like an old married

43

woman twice her age.

Hannah could hear Mr. Chambers' voice rolling out the door and hovering over the schoolyard like a fog. "Fifteen years ago there were only a few settlers in sixty square miles of woods. We had no choice but to help each other. If one family had a successful hunt, we'd share the meat. If another needed a house built, all the neighbors showed up and worked together. If there was sickness, we checked in on each other. We couldn't have survived alone. We need that same unity now.

"In the past few months we've lost four neighbors: Mrs. Parker, the Biltmores, the Sandersons, and old Mr. Peterson. The war has put new strains on our community, and if we want it to prosper, we must find a way to pull together and help our neighbors survive."

"I want to know what you expect me to do about it?" Hannah recognized Mrs. Clark's waspy voice. She was surprised the old tightwad even showed up.

"Of course no one expects you to act alone, Mrs. Clark. Our strength lies in numbers. There must be a way we can pool our resources and act together."

Hannah shut out the voices and wedged herself into a crevice where she could peek down through the branches unseen. She fancied herself a Yankee spy as she peered down at latecomers, filled with secret delight as they passed by unaware.

"Secret agent Melinda Dare," she whispered, "on assignment for General McClellan and in position above the assembly of rebel leaders. Officers are arriving singly and in groups. The enemy is now engaging in deep discussion over tactics for an invasion of Washington. Who will save the North from this new Southern aggression?

"But wait! Generals Longstreet and Jackson seem to be in disagreement. They are gesturing wildly, raising their voices. Lee is having a hard time mediating. Melinda Dare has been given the opportunity to act! If only she can break up the rebel meeting, Melinda Dare can save the country!"

Hannah pulled a handful of acorns from the tree and took aim. One by one she lobbed the grenades onto the roof of the schoolhouse. Moments later, General Lee himself dug out from under the rubble and staggered underneath her tree!

"Hannah," Joel called up to her, "Mama says you're flirting with Old Hickory."

She blew out an exasperated breath and dropped the rest of her ammunition on his head. She should have stayed home to fight with Justin.

Stretching out on her belly, she let her arms and legs dangle on either side of a stout limb. She could see Horatio stalking a mouse at the edge of the yard and knew Mr. Lawson was in the schoolhouse though she hadn't heard him speak yet. With nothing else to do, she listened to the voices drifting around her.

Mr. Stockdale's deep voice called out impatiently, "These are all nice gestures, but our neighbors are losing their farms. It's the crops that make or break them. If they can't get a harvest brought in and sold for a decent price, no charity organization you create will help."

"Then perhaps that is where can focus our efforts, William," Mr. Chambers suggested. "Perhaps we could form work groups and send each one to a struggling family."

"But who can spare the time to work two farms? With so few men to hire, we can hardly get our own crops in." That would be old Mr. Burgess, who was struggling without his sons.

An awkward silence fell. Most of the farmers were in the same situation.

Mr. Burgess continued, "I'm offering top wages to anybody who wants to hire on, and I'd suggest the same to others who want work done. I have to mind my own crops,

45

and I have neither the time nor inclination to work elsewhere for free."

The soft voice of a woman spoke up. "I'm in the same situation, Mr. Burgess. I'd be happy to pay for help, but there just aren't enough workers available. I have acres of corn and wheat standing in my fields, and if I can't turn them into cash, my land is at stake. My girls and I are working day and night."

Silence fell again, but this time it was thick with embarrassment. Hannah could imagine the men shuffling their feet and looking awkwardly about the room.

Finally Mr. Burgess broke the spell. "Shoot, Mrs. Perkins, you make a man eat his words!"

"I'm sorry, Mr. Burgess. That wasn't my intention."

"How about if I send my hired hands over for a day? It's not much, but it's all I can spare."

"I will pay them well, with gratitude."

Another silence. Then, "I could spare one day from my smithy."

"That's very kind of you, Mr. Stockdale."

Two others followed suit, and Mr. Chambers boomed out, "Well, that's fine. There are others who need help, and others who can spare a little. And if we work together the whole community will benefit."

Hannah was almost asleep from sheer boredom when Mr. Lawson's deep bass voice boomed out like a cannon and nearly knocked her off her branch. "I agree completely, Nelson! You folks have made me proud to live in such a community, and I'm compelled to join you, but in a different capacity. If, after the harvest, any of our neighbors are still facing financial difficulties, I would be willing to discuss the possibility of a few small loans."

There was another silence. "You taking up the banking business, Lawson?" Hannah could hear the skepticism in Mr. Stockdale's voice.

"The town could use it," someone replied. "Nearest bank is in Allegan."

The big man's laughter rolled out low and cheerful. "Nothing so large as that, but I have a bit put aside, and if it would stop another foreclosure, I'd like to invest it to help others."

"Well, it's mighty good of you, Mr. Lawson," someone said.

The buzz of voices droned on and Hannah lost interest. Darkness fell and mosquitoes began helping themselves to the exposed skin of her face and neck before she heard the first wagon rumble away. Below her the schoolhouse door spilled its occupants into the yard. She took a firm hold on her branch and swung easily down the tree, landing right next to Wes's mother.

"Land sakes, child!" Mrs. Carver exclaimed, her hands fluttering over her heart. "You do know how to startle a body!"

"Sorry, ma'am." Hannah grinned and started toward the farm cart.

"Wait a moment, Hannah. I'd like to speak with you," Mrs. Carver lowered her voice a notch, "about Mr. Covington."

Hannah drew in a breath. "Please don't tell my mother about my outburst."

"I did hear that," the woman chuckled. "He is a beastly man who deserved every word. However, you may want to reconsider your tune. He still wants you in his paintings."

Hannah thrust her chin out stubbornly. "Mrs. Carver, I have no intention of sitting for that... that...egotistical baboon!"

"I know he's no prize to work for, but he has a few wealthy patrons. And he's offered to pay you hard money for your time."

Hannah's eyes flashed blue steel. "Thank you for tell-

47

ing me, ma'am, but I will have to be destitute before I go crawling to that man for wages."

Mrs. Carver patted her hand. "It's your decision, dear. I won't say a word."

Chapter Six

A hoot owl called from the tangles behind the barn, though it was only late afternoon. The sun was still skewered to the tops of the trees like an apple on a garden post.

Wes's signal.

Hannah glanced cautiously around the barnyard. Only a few chickens scratched at the weedy patches. She scooted behind the barn.

"Get all your work done?" Wes asked. He wore a pair of stained buckskins that were a little too big and carried an ancient Kentucky longrifle. The gun stood as tall as Hannah. It had elegant lines and a carved stock worn smooth as fine silk. Wes's grandfather had carried the old flintlock over the Appalachian Mountains, and it was now affectionately named "Ol' Joe" in honor of the pioneer. Across Wes's chest hung a powder horn and a pouch of bullets.

Hannah moaned. She'd been cutting wheat all week using a cradle scythe sized for a grown man then stacking the heavy sheaves into shocks so they would be protected from moisture. Her arms, her shoulders, and her back ached, and the harvest wasn't half finished.

"Chores are never done. Mama's down with the ague

again. She won't know I'm gone." But they'd have to avoid Joel and Justin, who never left the field before black night.

They skedaddled for the woods. Most of the land roundabouts had been harvested for lumber, though second growth forest reclaimed any area not tilled under. About a mile east of the farm, however, between two arms of the Rabbit River, a stand of old timber that had escaped the lumberman's ax still stood. It was toward this copse that the children directed their steps.

They crossed fields surrounded by rail fences. It was common practice to let livestock run wild in the woods. Why waste good feed on animals that could forage for themselves? Pigs, horses, cows, even sheep were rounded up and pastured when autumn brought harsher weather. The fences weren't built to hold animals in the fields, but to keep them out. But as the land settled up, more and more folks began to complain about the wandering animals.

In the distance they spotted a figure standing beside a tripod.

"Is that Mr. Covington?" Hannah questioned, squinting at the figure.

"Probably. I heard him tell Pa he was going sketching today."

"He's still at the hotel?"

"Only until Mrs. Clark's boarder moves out. Then she gets him."

"I hope he gets bit by a massasauga rattlesnake!"

Wes laughed. "Living with that old battle-ax would be more fitting punishment, don't you think?"

She giggled. "He and Mrs. Clark are perfect for each other!"

Soon the homesteads gave way to wild, swampy forest. Mosquitoes flew so thick Hannah breathed them in, but the woods also harbored deer, rabbit, coon, and squirrel. Pa used to bring her here when she was small. Back then, every

50

shadow became a panther or an Indian, but today an entire regiment of Rebels hid among the trees.

They waded the river and Hannah dropped behind a large rock. "General McClellan," she ordered, "Take your men around to the right and close in on the rebel's flank. I'll go to the left and catch them in a cross fire."

Wes moved to obey then spun back around. "I'd rather be Grant."

"I'm General Grant."

Wes grinned and saluted. He began creeping away, the long upright rifle barrel marking his progress.

Hannah found a fallen branch to serve as a weapon. Keeping her eyes on Wes, she skirted the woods to his left, stopping on occasion to take out enemy soldiers.

Suddenly Wes cried out, "Cavalry! Coming up the hill behind us!"

The friends closed ranks and engaged the enemy shoulder to shoulder until they drove the last rider off the hill. Then, laughing and panting, they slouched against a massive tree trunk. When her breathing regulated, Hannah let her head flop back and closed her eyes.

"You look pretty done in," Wes observed. "Sure you're up for this?"

"Shoot," she scorned, "I feel better than I have all week."

Wes grinned. "That's what I like about you. You're never afraid to loosen up and have a little fun. Not like some old stuffed shirts I can think of."

"Like who?"

"Well, my father, for one."

"And Sue Ellen! Can you picture her running through the brambles?"

"Only if there's a spelling bee on the other side."

Hannah laughed. "Have you heard from Marcus lately?"

"Not since he got hurt, but I'm not worried. His letter said the bullet only grazed his arm. He's probably sipping tea in some hospital, amusing pretty nurses with tales of his bravery. Won't be long till they kick him out and send him back after the Johnnies."

"I hope that's all it is," she said.

Their conversation lagged, and Hannah could hear the rustle of some small animal in the dry grass to her left. She jumped up. "Here they come again!"

They ducked behind the tree as another company of horses swept their lines.

"There's too many of them! General Grant, we must fall back!"

Step by step, the children gave up their hard-fought ground, retreating to the shelter of a fallen log from which they took out rebel officers one by one until the regiment fled in confusion. A pair of squirrels lectured them from above, and one old porcupine peered down at them from a hollow in a tree.

Hannah slumped in relief. "Any casualties, general?"

"I don't believe so." Wes propped his gun on end. "We've shot enough rebs. Time for some critters."

He climbed onto a stump to reach the top of the long barrel and carefully loaded the rifle. Unscrewing the cap, he tapped out a measure of powder from the horn and poured it down the barrel. Then he wrapped a bullet in a greased cloth and drove it to the bottom of the barrel with the ramrod. Finally, he poured a bit of powder in the firing pan and cocked the hammer. The old fellow was ready to fire.

"General Grant, would you like the first shot?" he asked, holding out the gun.

Hannah accepted it.

The woods were full of small game, but Hannah had a hankering for squirrel stew. As she scanned the treetops for the fox squirrels that had berated them moments before, she realized how shadowy the woods had become.

"We battled too long, General McClellan. It's getting hard to see."

"Best time of day to spot deer."

But Hannah didn't want venison; she wanted squirrel. She continued to search the limbs above.

"It used to be dangerous outside after dark," she remarked. "One time a pack of wolves sent my pa up a tree only a quarter mile from our door. Mama heard him yelling and came to his rescue with a gun slung around her neck and a burning brand in each hand."

"Your ma did that?"

Hannah nodded. "When Seth was a baby. Pa says she shot one of the wolves. Got a ten dollar bounty and sold the hide, too."

Wes glanced uneasily at the shadows forming around them. "Glad they're not around anymore."

A movement in the tree caught her eye, and Hannah raised the rifle to her shoulder. The motion felt like a dance, performed with perfect step and balance. She aimed at the squirrel, but just as she applied pressure to the trigger, a crash sounded in the underbrush behind them.

Hannah whipped the gun about, aiming for the noise. Wes had dropped behind the fallen tree. Only something huge made a clamor like that. And she had just one shot.

The rustling inched closer, skirting the edge of the clearing. Hannah followed the sound with the gun's muzzle. A breathless moment later, a black bear emerged from the brush and strolled through the meadow. He was young—nothing as big as the hide hanging in the hotel—and fat and rolling after a summer of feeding. With an easy flick of his paw he turned over a rock and nosed underneath.

Hannah steadied her hands and carefully aimed the gun.

"Don't shoot!" Wes hissed. "The caliber isn't enough

53

to kill it!"

She kept the gun trained on the bruin. If it decided to charge, she was dang sure going to slow it down!

The bear wandered into a nearby thicket and began munching on berries. After half a minute, it caught wind of the children. Grunting once, it rose on its hind legs, snuffled the air, and stared through the gloom directly at Hannah. She locked eyes with it, every muscle tensed to shoot.

But the bear must have decided she didn't pose much of a threat. It dropped to all fours and wandered back into the woods, stopping to nose beneath a fallen log for one last mouthful.

Wes stood up shakily, and Hannah lowered the gun. Only then did she notice her heart exploding beneath her ribs. Wait till she wrote to Seth about this!

"Shall we head home?" Wes sounded a little rattled.

But Hannah had spotted a squirrel. In one easy motion, she lifted the gun, sighted down the long barrel, and pulled the trigger. The rodent dropped to the forest floor like a dishrag.

"Now I'm ready," she stated, handing him the rifle.

She stuffed her kill into a gunny sack and followed Wes back to the river where they came upon a whole settlement of squirrels. Wes reloaded and doubled their catch, and together they clambered over another fence.

As they swung out of the woods, Hannah found her reckoning of time not as inaccurate as she had feared. The sun had not set, rather it was cowering behind a heavy bank of clouds that drenched the county in early twilight. The cold wind rushing ahead of it tasted wet.

Lightning licked at the clouds, and heavy peals of thunder rumbled like a distant locomotive. The children began to run. They nearly beat the storm, but at the very edge of the farm the sky opened up and cast down hard, cold pellets.

"Hail!" Hannah yelled and dashed for the old log cabin, only a stone's throw away. "Follow me!"

Plink! Plink! Plink! The ice dropped sparingly at first then multiplied with a rush that stung their backs and rattled the dry grass.

They gained the shelter of the building, watching gravely as the marbles bounced through the fields like a swarm of white locust. Pumpkins and potatoes would escape damage, but the hail flattened the unharvested wheat, driving the precious grains into the ground. Visions of new shoes and new bonnets rose from the tattered field like spirits of dead dreams.

When the falling ice melted into a downpour, the children raced across the slippery yard and into the gathering room where the entire Wallace family had congregated. Ma was out of bed, looking strained but no longer sweating or shivering. Joel stood apart, watching the storm out the window, and Justin stared sullenly into the fire. Not one word was uttered about Hannah's long absence or the gunny sack in her hand.

Only Maddy seemed not to notice the ruined crop. She beamed at Hannah. "I'm going to have a baby!"

Stunned, Hannah's eyes flicked over Mama's pale face that struggled to express all the joy and loss thrust on her within a few moments' time. Her glance bobbled over the boys and finally found an anchor in the solid bulk of Doctor Graves, the town physician.

He nodded. "I expect a new arrival sometime in March."

Hannah gaped at her sister, who looked like she'd just been given a thousand dollars. She couldn't imagine being happy about a baby at sixteen, but she realized Maddy's whole life had been leading up to this moment. From baby dolls to doe-eyed crushes and finally her crazy marriage to Tommy, it was what she always wanted. And she'd probably be a very good mother. At least she'd have someone else to boss around.

"Congratulations," Hannah said out loud. But inside she resolved to never tie herself down while she still had so much living to do.

Chapter Seven

The whole family gleaned in the field for days, working to save everything they could from the flattened crop. It was backbreaking work, even harder than working the scythe. They crawled over the field, stooping to retrieve broken stalks off the ground, gathering them into bundles, and forming them into shocks. Many of the stalks had every single grain beaten off and ground into the dirt, but they recovered anything they could.

Hannah stopped to stretch her aching back. "I hate this farm! I wish I could run away."

"Where would you go?" Justin scorned. "No one else would have you."

"I'd take my chances just to get away from you."

"The way you've been shirking, nobody would miss you," he accused. "A lot more could have been harvested before the storm if you weren't always cutting out early."

Hannah felt heat staining her cheeks. "You think you're so important. You're not worth half as much as you think you are."

Joel stepped in before the fight got out of hand. "Justin, you will be a man in time, but less of one if you keep

57

squabbling with girls. Hannah, you're stuck here so make the most of it. There's nothing either of you could have done to save this crop."

But Justin was right and Hannah knew it. She had skipped out on work. Maybe if she had tried harder, if she had worked longer, if she had stayed home with the boys that last afternoon things might be different. But it was too late. The crop would only fetch half its worth and she alone was to blame.

She should have stayed. She should have worked like another son for Pa.

When they went inside, after the last of the wheat stood in sheaves bowing to the sun's hot, drying rays, Hannah ventured the nerve to ask, "Mama, how much money do we owe?"

"Joel?" Mama asked wearily, sinking into her rocking chair in the gathering room.

Joel sat in Pa's seat on the other side with his feet stretched to the fireplace. "Won't know for certain till I get this wheat sold. But it's more than we can pay without next year's crop."

"Why on earth did Pa borrow so much?" Maddy blurted out in frustration, toppling the mending basket on her lap.

Joel shrugged. "What else could he do when ends didn't meet? But he figured on being out from under the debt this year, and the bank is expecting payment."

Hannah automatically reached for the carding paddles. "What happens if we can't pay?" she asked, combing the woolen fibers almost without thought.

"We will pay," Mama insisted.

"But what if we don't?"

"Pa put the farm up as collateral," Joel admitted.

Hannah's eyes grew huge, and she saw her fear reflected in Justin's eyes. What would Pa think if they lost his farm?

"I don't want you kids to worry about this," Mama insisted. "Joel and I will go to Allegan to sort it out. If the bank will give us till spring we can pay it off then."

"How?" Maddy scoffed. "By planting crops in October? We might as well give them the farm right now."

Justin jumped up, fists doubled at his sides. "Shut up, Maddy! You could have helped if you hadn't spent all the money Tommy sent you on material for new dresses."

"It's my money!" Maddy yelled back. "And I need new dresses. I'm going to split these seams in a few weeks."

"All your money?" Justin asked skeptically.

"That's enough," Mama commanded. "We have vegetables to put by for winter, and we'll have pork enough after we slaughter the hog. We can last a long time without needing anything from the store. And there's your father's pay and the money from butter, eggs, and wool."

"That should pay it off in four or five years," Maddy drawled sarcastically.

"And if Maddy continues to live with us," Mama added with a pointed lift of her brow, "she can pay room and board out of her husband's check."

Maddy harrumphed.

"Mama," Joel said hesitantly, looking down at his bare feet. He hadn't been able to squeeze them into his shoes for three months, and they stuck out four inches past the hem of his trousers.

Mama sighed. "Of course that won't do for winter. I don't suppose you fit in Seth's clothes?"

"These are Seth's," he mumbled, turning red.

"Then take your father's boots and I'll alter his trousers. Everyone else can make do." Mama looked at each of them and smiled. "We'll be fine. We're Wallaces." And that's all she would allow on the subject.

59

The next morning Rounder took the planks at an easy canter, his neck arching gracefully, his ears alert and swiveling. Hannah clung to his back as easily as the cockleburs stuck in his mane. She sat astride, the skirt of her best dress hiked over her knees.

Her heart felt lighter now that she had come up with a way to redeem herself, to make up for some of her part in losing the wheat. But she so dreaded the task she had assigned herself that even on her way to accomplish it she drew back, swerving off the toll road. She cantered through a mown field, letting her horse and her imagination lead her elsewhere.

A haze, as if from a thousand cook fires, shrouded the trees at the edge of the field. The Confederate camp! It must lay over the crest of the hill, the men just rising for breakfast. She had chosen a risky path, but she had information that must reach General Grant.

An imagined shot rang out, rolling over the grassy field. Catching the flash of a sentry's uniform from behind a stone fence, she urged Rounder to greater speed. Another shot, and a minie ball whizzed past her ear. Rounder raced down a gentle slope and into the safety of a copse of trees.

Hannah let the horse have its head. It leaped over a small brook and swept out across another open field. She delighted in the freedom of the wind whipping past her face. She threw her head back and laughed out loud.

Suddenly she heard the sound of hoofbeats pounding behind her. Looking back, she spotted a mounted patrol bearing down on her, pistols drawn. The enemy had discovered her and was chasing her down!

She kicked Rounder hard. The obedient horse flew over the field, neck low, tail streaming. Hannah held on, barely able to see through the black mane lashing her face.

Powerful legs pounded the dirt like pistons. Hooves kicked up great chunks of earth. The deep chest heaved with mighty gasps.

Hannah thrilled with the swiftness of the chase, urging the horse to its top speed. She circled a cornfield, following it around a barn where she startled an old farmer who shouted at her and shook a pitchfork.

Her daydream broken, Hannah slowed at the Hilliards crossroads and turned back toward Wayland. Rounder snorted and tossed his head just to prove he wasn't spent and covered the four miles at an easy jog. Thirty minutes later, Hannah tied him to the hitching rail in front of Mr. Lawson's store, cooled and recovered. Then she tramped across the road to Mrs. Clark's house, smoothed out her skirts, and forced herself to knock at the door.

The old woman answered and glared down at her suspiciously. "What do you want?"

Hannah squared her shoulders. "I've come to speak with Mr. Covington."

Mrs. Clark narrowed her eyelids. "You know I don't allow children to disturb my boarders."

Hannah bit back her annoyance. "He asked to speak with me. I received word through Mrs. Carver."

At the old woman's skeptical frown, Hannah continued, "Please, just tell him I'm here."

Without a word, Mrs. Clark shut the door in her face.

Hannah blew out a frustrated sigh and paced in front of the house, not at all certain the woman would deliver her message. A few moments later, however, the curtain moved at the window and Mr. Covington peered out.

Hannah took a deep breath. For her father's sake and the sake of her family she must swallow her dignity.

The door opened and the gruff old man stepped outside. "So you're back. I thought you might be."

Hannah fought down her irritation. "Mr. Covington,"

61

she said through stiff lips, "I must apologize for my past behavior. It was wrong of me to speak to you as I did."

Mr. Covington let out a sound like the snorting of a horse. "I expected no better in this backwoods town."

Hannah's nostrils flared. "I beg your forgiveness," she managed, "and I have reconsidered my decision. I would like to sit for your pictures. Mrs. Carver hinted that we might come to an understanding."

He drew a pipe and a pouch of tobacco out of his pocket. He took the time to fill and light his pipe then he pointed it at her. "Miss Wallace, you will find that I do not mince words. I expect this same clarity in others. Now, come out and say exactly what you mean."

Hannah could feel heat building under the bodice of her dress, and she could barely form the words. "All right," she snapped. "If you want me to sit for your paintings, you will have to pay me."

"That's better," he grunted, squinting at her through a wreath of smoke. "Then let us reach this understanding, as you called it. I need a model. I do not need a critic. I do not need a student. I do not even need a companion. If you can contain yourself to this capacity, you will be generously compensated after each session."

He took a silver coin out of his pocket and flicked it, sparkling, into the air before palming it again.

Hannah could barely contain her contempt. She lifted her chin and glared proudly down her nose at him. "I can."

He grinned beneath his beard and pocketed the money. "Then I think, Miss Wallace, that we do understand each other. Please come in."

As they entered, Mrs. Clark scurried away from the door where she had been eavesdropping. To cover her embarrassment, she snapped, "Don't take that pipe into my house, Mr. Covington. I simply will not allow it."

"Nonsense," he countered. "I'm just passing through.

The girl and I will take our work into the backyard where I will have adequate light. And since you are already sufficiently familiar with our business, I needn't say anything further."

Indignant, the woman clicked her teeth together like a snapping turtle and sashayed into the kitchen. Hannah pinched off a grin. The exchange made up for some of her humiliation.

"Follow me," Mr. Covington ordered. "Help me carry some things."

He led Hannah up the stairs and into a simply furnished room. The bed, bureau, and washstand congregated haphazardly on one side. The other side held a dozen half-finished canvases that reclined on easels or leaned against the wall in various states of repose. Paper sketches littered the furniture and blanketed the floor like a dusting of snow.

Hannah studied the pictures as the artist collected his tools. In one sketch she recognized a gnarled old willow tree that stood in the park square. Another showed the Wayland House. Barns, gardens, cows, machinery sitting idle in fields—the canvases held scenes she passed every day, but they looked different somehow, romantic and inviting.

Mr. Covington dismissed the landscapes with a wave of his hand, much as he had dismissed her the first time they met. "Drivel," he grunted. "Folks surrounded by concrete and steel will pay a decent sum for a view of the country-side. It earns my bread. But a face can tell a story, and yours, my dear, speaks volumes."

They wrestled the artist's supplies down the steps and out the back door where Mr. Covington moved Hannah about the yard for ten minutes, posing her one way then another, trying different lighting, different angles. At last, he ordered her to stand still, head tilted slightly, face expressionless, staring into the distance with a milk pail—borrowed from Mr. Lawson—clasped in front of her.

Mr. Covington disappeared behind the canvas. "Do you always dress like that?" he asked.

"Like what?"

"Like you're heading off to Sunday school. That dress fits to a proper length and the lace is still white. I'd wager you put on the only decent dress you own just make a good impression. Am I correct?" He popped his head over the canvas and gave her a frank stare.

The man was so infuriating!

"Mr. Covington," she ground out, "if you've sent for me just to ridicule me, you would have done better to stay in your city. Here, folks have to work for their living six days a week. We only go to church once. So explain why I should own more than one good dress."

He took a long drag on his pipe, eyed her evenly, and changed the subject. "Your daddy farms?"

She tossed her hair. "He does."

"Carver told me he's off fighting."

"Yes."

He disappeared behind the canvas again. "Seen action?"

"I don't know. He's only been gone five weeks."

"He will soon enough, God help him. The fools in Washington will see to that. They sacrifice men like Passover lambs." He muttered darkly about an "inept bureaucracy" and "desktop warriors" and the politicians who had brought the war on, especially Michigan's own senator, Zachariah Chandler.

"The great fool called for a little bloodletting," he grumbled, "without having any idea what war is about. Well, he's getting it now, by golly. He's getting it now!"

Hannah didn't like this vein of conversation any better than the last one. She was tired of doomsayers and their negativity, and she was just about out of patience with arrogant artists as well. After pressing her lips together for many long minutes, she finally burst out, "Mr. Covington, you've made your views quite plain, but you're no more a soldier than I am. What makes you such an expert on this matter?"

His head popped up from behind the painting, and he regarded her shrewdly. Finally, he spoke. "Miss Wallace, if I paint your face as I see it before me now, not a man in a million will purchase it."

With an effort, Hannah wiped the impatience from her features. For two hours she stood stiffly and quietly, and Mr. Covington seemed content to paint in silence. At last the artist laid three coins in her hand, but as she turned to go, he stopped her. "Miss Wallace, there's no reason under heaven that you should own two Sunday dresses. And even less to wear one here. I'm painting you as a farm girl. Dress like one."

Her resentment rose to her cheeks again, and she whisked away without even a glance at the canvas.

Chapter Eight

The next week, Joel hitched Rounder to the cart, and he and Mama drove out of the yard before the sun rose. Hannah watched them go, wishing she could have gone too. She'd only been to Allegan once, a long time ago. She remembered streets lined on both sides with buildings and sleek steamships cruising the wide, strong currents of the Kalamazoo. She desperately wished to see it all again, but too much work waited at home.

She and Justin spent the day threshing. First they beat the dried wheat with long flails to separate the grain from the stalk. Then the grain had to be winnowed. Each child took hold of opposite ends of an old bedsheet and tossed the heavy kernels between them, allowing the lighter chaff to blow away in the breeze. It was long, exhausting work, but they could no longer afford to hire Yancey's machine.

The cart returned hours after supper, and Hannah could see the discouragement in Mama's eyes. She knew Joel's words before he spoke.

"The bank refused us. The fellow said an extension would be poor business practice, that no woman alone could ever hope to repay it."

Justin bristled. "Didn't you tell him she wouldn't be alone? She has two men working the farm."

"Course I told him, but he didn't see it our way. Without Pa and Seth here, he wasn't willing to take the gamble."

"It's no gamble at all," Hannah insisted. "They've already loaned the money. All we need is a little more time to pay it back."

"I said that, too, but it wasn't any good. We have thirty days."

Mama's face looked tight, like a woolen dress washed in too-hot water. "It's just a setback. We still have several loads of potatoes and the pumpkin crop to sell. And we can part with the sheep and the calf. Joel will round them up tomorrow."

"We could sell off the north pasture to Mr. Patton," Joel hesitated. "Won't be long and the law will make him pen that herd, even in summer."

Mama pursed her lips with the same determination that carried her to the wilderness so many years ago. "Let's try everything else first. In the meantime, there is much to be done."

That was the honest truth. Along with everyday chores, there were apples to dry, more potatoes to fork, the garden to harvest and store, a field of pumpkins to be picked and cured, more hay to stack, the livestock to round up, walnuts to gather, and fall had only begun.

But Mama didn't allow any work on the Sabbath. And every third Sunday, when Reverend Whelan rotated into Wayland from his other congregations, the family dutifully squeezed into the red schoolhouse for the Methodist service.

This week excitement ran especially high, because after the service there was to be a community social with the Congregational church including a potluck, a ballgame, and visiting that would go on till evening services. Several ladies had also organized a bandage drive to benefit the army.

Mama hustled everyone out of the house, instructing Joel to carry the heavy hamper and Hannah to fetch along the sewing scissors and a pair of old linens.

The air felt cool and clear as they walked to town. All around them the land was shedding its summer garments for the glowing tones of autumn. Crisp mornings had stained the trees red and yellow at their fingertips, and a few early leaves cascaded to earth when the wind touched them. The same breeze rattled the brown cornstalks and turned fields long saturated with hot, yellow rays into waves of molten gold.

Reverend Whelan performed at his fiery best. After his final amen, the congregation flowed from the schoolhouse like cattle released from a winter paddock. Maddy squealed and rushed to share her good news with a knot of girl-friends. Justin found Peter Patton, and the two were soon up the nearest tree shooting acorns down at their friends with Peter's slingshot. Even Joel ambled off to join a school chum, drawing veiled glances from Sue Ellen.

Hannah greeted Sue Ellen politely and hustled to join Wes at the front of the food line.

Wes grinned. "I wish I could carry five plates. Look at all this food!"

Long plank tables sagged beneath the weight of dozens of dishes. Ham, venison, roasted pigeon, fried chicken, mounds of mashed potatoes, bowls of corn dripping with butter, tomato slices, baskets towering with fluffy biscuits, apple pie, pumpkin pie, and blackberry pie. Hannah's mouth watered as if she were an old hound snuffling outside a rabbit hole.

"Any news from your Pa?" Wes asked.

"We got a letter last week. He's in Washington DC. Seth said they're training in arms."

Seth always wrote about what the regiment was doing, but Pa filled his letters with descriptions of the places he'd seen. He told of the blue, smoky haze of the mountains that rolled one on top of another until she felt she could feel the damp droplets on her cheek. He described streams that fluttered like white ribbons down cliffs of sheer black rock. She could picture the great Horseshoe Bend, where the track wound in such a circle that the head of the train nearly bit its own tail as it wound through the hills. And she could feel the weight and strength of the wide Susquehanna River pushing itself to the sea. She knew Pa painted the pictures just for her, and they felt too private to share even with Wes.

She was saved by Reverend Whelan, who called for silence and blessed the meal.

The rumble of voices resumed all around her. As she filled her plate, Hannah could hear Mr. Carver conversing with Mr. Lawson.

"Of course you're in no hurry to have the railroad come through," Mr. Lawson said. "The hotel sits right on the toll road, and it's raking in business from the stage. But a railroad will benefit the rest of us. When it comes, it will turn Wayland into a real town, not some little frontier way station."

"Apparently it's the railroad that's in no hurry," Mr. Carver answered. "Rumors have circulated for fifteen years about a line linking Kalamazoo and Grand Rapids."

"True, but the Grand Rapids and Indiana railroad company has formed with that very objective in mind."

"They formed eight years ago," Carver scoffed. "By the time they actually lay down track, I'll be too deaf to hear the train."

Lawson chuckled, but he wouldn't be deterred. "It's only a matter of time, Isaiah. And when it comes, the railroad will run right through Wayland, and every square foot of real estate in this town will triple in value."

"Amazing machine, the railroad." Doctor Graves spoke up from the food line across the table. "Never thought

I'd live to see such wonders. Now I can't imagine running this war without it."

"Blast this war!" Mr. Carver frowned. Every conversation, it seemed, turned to it eventually.

The doctor replied, "Don't be too quick to judge, Isaiah. It's keeping our nation together."

"It's ripping it apart, and I've had a year and a half to form my judgment," Mr. Carver contradicted. "It has inflated prices, driven up taxes, siphoned off our work force, and provided a thousand opportunities for unscrupulous characters."

Doctor Graves frowned thoughtfully. "Every war requires sacrifice. The Union is the greatest nation ever created. Our grandfathers knew the value of liberty. They knew life without it. They fought to create a nation where religion, wealth, and race don't matter. They sacrificed for its creation. We must not let it disintegrate."

"The Union isn't worth the price we're paying for it." Mr. Covington joined the conversation. Hannah had sat for him two more times, and each had felt as stilted and awkward as the first. She hustled to stay well ahead of him in line.

"So what if it breaks up?" the artist continued. "The Confederates are our kin. They share our religion and our style of government, or stories, our history. If we had let them go, eventually they would have come back. Or at least become our closest ally. I agree with Carver. This disagreement is sucking the blood out of both sides."

Hannah and Wes carried their meals under a scarlet maple tree. They were too busy eating to talk, but not to listen. The cluster of men stood nearby, their conversation drawing more and more participants.

Mr. Stockdale joined in. "I think we can all agree it was the South that started this here conflict. With their high-falutin' ways and their squabble over slavery, what choice did they give us?"

"Neither side was without guilt, William," Doctor Graves admonished. "North and South have both been pressing the slavery issue for decades."

"And we certainly couldn't ignore it any longer," Reverend Whelan emphasized. "A society that allows one man's possession of another must be reprimanded."

"Hold on there, preacher," Mr. Stockdale objected. "My son ain't fighting for no darkies."

Mr. Carver waved a fork at the crowd. "Even slavery would have died of its own accord. It's become unaffordable. More and more Southern lawmakers have been pushing to ban it. The issue would have resolved itself soon enough."

"There are three million men with black skin who wouldn't agree with you," the reverend interjected quietly.

Just then, Johnny Wilson trotted through the park with an armload of sawmill slabs, and boys scurried from all directions like ants drawn to spilled food. Someone produced a cowhide ball, and several leather catching pads appeared out of nowhere.

"Going to play?" Hannah asked Wes.

"Course I am!" He bolted the rest of his food and handed her his empty plate.

As he jogged away, she clutched the plate with thinly veiled disgust. She was nobody's servant, and certainly not his wife! Maddy might have chosen such a life of service, but not Hannah.

She left his plate beside the tree.

After stowing her own plate safely in her mother's hamper, Hannah marched to the ball diamond where the boys hustled to squeeze in a game before the men finished their conversation and took over the field. She'd teach Wes a lesson and prove to every boy on that ball field that she was nobody's housemaid, least of all Wes Carver's.

She waited patiently until Wes stood up to bat. She watched him miss the first ball, nick the next one a glancing blow, and finally strike out on a third pitch. While the fellows were still ribbing him over his poor performance, Hannah timed her entrance and took the bat slab out of his hands.

"My turn," she announced.

The boys stopped laughing and stared at her with a mixture of surprise and hesitation. Wes's mouth popped open nearly wide enough to catch a frog. "Are you serious?"

"Why not?" she asked. "It doesn't look that difficult."

He crossed his arms and smirked. "This I've got to see."

She ignored him. "Sammy Davis," she yelled, threatening the pitcher with the wooden slab, "if you don't pitch that ball to me, I'm going to lock you in the outhouse tomorrow at recess!"

With obvious reluctance, he wound up for the pitch.

Hannah braced herself. "Give me your dirty plate, will you?" she muttered to Wes.

The ball zoomed past and the bat whistled. A clean miss.

"Strike one!" A few snickers sounded out in the field.

"Throw another!" she yelled.

Again, the ball flew past and she connected with thin air.

"One more and you're out," Sammy told her.

She nodded and took a firmer grip on the bat. Sammy wound up, and the pitch rocketed toward her. Time seemed to slow. She focused, watching the ball inch closer and closer. Her muscles tensed. She swung hard.

Swish!

The ball dropped to the ground behind her. She missed again.

Every movement on the field stilled. The boys watched

her uncertainly, not knowing how she'd respond, but Wes had no such hesitation. He was doubled over, hooting so loudly he could barely catch his breath.

His backside was nearest to her. With a smart little smile, she stepped forward, took careful aim, and swung with all her might. The board connected with a loud slap that sent Wes sprawling across home plate.

"Grand slam!" Sammy cried as laughter exploded across the field. Hannah calmly handed the board to the next boy in line.

A group of ladies, including Hannah's mother, had settled themselves near the ball field where they could watch the game as they tore old linens into strips. They had all seen Hannah's performance. Most turned politely to their work as she approached, but Mrs. Clark looked downright scandalized. Old grouch.

Mrs. Carver chuckled with amusement, her apple cheeks round and red, and slid over to make room for her. "Hannah Wallace, I declare, what is your mother going to do with you?"

Hannah beamed at the woman then at her mother, whose lips pressed together in a firm line. She knew she'd get a talking to on the way home, but it had been worth it.

She picked up one of the bandages and wrapped it around and around her fingers, forming it into a compact roll. The smooth white strips flowed over her skin and she found it difficult to picture them soaked with blood. Somewhere, she knew, there must be hospitals for the wounded men. Elton Brewster had come back from the war with a patch over one eye. And Danny Woodrow's older brother, Nick, had a bullet go right through his shoulder. She'd seen the scar herself. Both wounds must have been wrapped in similar cloths, crimson with their blood. But Nick rejoined the army as soon as he was able, and Mr. Brewster could still plow his fields as good as any two-eyed man. And

Hannah could hardly imagine the bandages any color but white.

"How is Maddy faring?" Mrs. Carver asked Mama. "Has she been ill?"

"Some." Mama glanced over at her oldest daughter who sat among her girlfriends teasing and taunting the young men taking over the ball field. "She's so young. I don't think she really understands what all this is going to mean."

"To think a married woman would act in such a way," Mrs. Clark clucked. "Amelia, I'm shocked that you are sitting here watching her behavior. Go speak to her!"

Mama sighed and ripped another long strip. "She'll grow up soon enough, Edith."

Mrs. Carver cut her eyes over to Mama. "And how are you holding up to this pregnancy, Grandma?"

Mama smiled. Then she giggled. "I'm much too young to be a grandmother, you know."

"Of course you are! Weren't we just girls ourselves?"

The women fell to reminiscing about their own childhoods, spent in different states far away. Everyone in Michigan came from somewhere else. The state hadn't even existed when they were young.

Mama looked livelier than she had in weeks. Years fell from her face, and her cheeks glowed rosy with health. But their conversation was interrupted by Mr. Chambers, who jogged into the gathering waving a newspaper in his hand. "The *Record* just came on the stage. Lincoln has set the slaves free!"

In the stunned silence, the ball fell dead on the playing field. Then excitement broke over the park square, covering it like a wave, soaking it in sound. Everyone spoke at once.

"That'll teach those traitors!"

"About time the North showed some decisive action."

"How we gunna enforce such a thing? We can't even

74

keep the Union together."

Hannah heard Mr. Stockdale's voice rise above the others. "I won't have no part of freeing any darkies! Abe just lost hisself a volunteer."

The blur of noise swelled and merged until one shouted question brought it to a swift close. "Where's the Confederate army, Nelson?"

Since Bull Run three weeks ago, the papers had reported that Confederate General Robert Lee had crossed the Susquehanna River and taken the war into northern territory. There had been mention of engagements, but fact and rumor flowed together like mud and water.

Mr. Chambers read aloud in his deep voice, "'The Maryland campaign continued as Lee pushed farther onto Union soil. Federal troops stationed at Harper's Ferry were surrounded by a Confederate division and surrendered on September 15. Meanwhile, McClellan repelled further divisions in a series of battles on South Mountain on the 14th.'"

That had been more than a week ago, Hannah realized.

"'Lee fell back to Sharpsburg. Instead of pressing his advantage, McClellan allowed the southern army to regroup before he attacked at Antietam Creek on September 17. His hesitation may have resulted in the bloodiest day of America's history, with astounding casualties on both sides, though statistics cannot be conclusive at this time.'"

Mr. Stockdale spit in the dirt with disgust. "McClellan has all the gumption of a maiden aunt. Lincoln better find a general who knows how to fight before this one leaches the life out of our army."

"Read the casualty roll, Nelson," someone called over muttered agreement.

Mr. Chambers turned the page and scanned the list of names before he began reading. "'First Michigan Infantry,

Company A: First Lieutenant Willis Harrelson, shot through shoulder; Charles Parsons, leg amputated; Sergeant Samuel Mulligan, killed—'"

Hannah blocked out his voice as it droned on and on; there were just too many names to absorb. Instead she focused on her mother, noticing the fine lines spreading from the corners of her eyes like cracks in plaster. Mama's fingers were interwoven so tightly with those of Mrs. Carver they had turned bone white. Hannah had once seen such an expression of intense concentration on a barn cat just before it sprang on a mouse.

At last, far down the page, Mr. Chambers reached the Seventeenth, her father's regiment, and she turned her attention back with an unfamiliar prickle of apprehension.

"'—Company D: Charles Denny, killed; Daniel Forrester, head wound; Edward Blake, arm; Ralph Douglass, killed; Seth Wallace, finger—'"

A finger! Seth had lost a finger! She laughed out loud in her relief, drawing daggers of reproach from those around her. What a whopping story Seth would have to tell when he got home. She almost envied him. She was so delighted she almost missed the rest of the roll.

"'—Orvil Peterson, killed; Benjamin Ross, killed; Tommy Stockdale, killed; George Hess, arm amputated—'"

A scream brought Hannah back to her senses. Maddy had collapsed, her body pooling in a lifeless puddle on the grass. Mama rushed to her, merged with her into a miserable heap, stroked her hair if she were still a little girl.

Not Tommy!

A smoky haze touched Hannah's eyes, burning them, blurring them. It couldn't be Tommy. Not Tommy, with his mischievous wink and his impish grin, with his baby on the way.

Suddenly Sue Ellen was beside her, propping her up, sliding an arm around her waist. Hannah leaned into her.

Had Tommy even known he was going to be a father? What was Maddy going to do without him?

Her tears flowed then. Filling her. Flooding her.

Through a watery veil, she saw Mr. Stockdale trying to comfort his wife, not an ounce of bluster left in him. His son, it seemed, wouldn't be fighting for any darkies after all.

Chapter Nine

"Why, Molly, what a pleasant surprise!" Mama exclaimed when she opened the door to her neighbor's knock. "Come in! Would you like a cup of tea?" She signaled to Hannah to put the kettle on the stove.

"Thank you, Amelia, but I really can't stay. I just—"

Justin popped his head in the doorway, his hands still wrapped with the yarn Mama had been winding into a ball. "Did Peter come with you?"

"Justin!" Mama scolded. "You know better than to interrupt."

"Sorry, Mama."

Mrs. Patton smiled hesitantly. "Peter's at home finishing his chores, which brings me to the reason for my call. You see, my husband usually rounds up our horses in October." She paused.

Mama put a hand on her arm. "No bad news, I hope?"

"Oh, no! Josiah's fine. His enlistment will be up in another month. It's just that I hate to come asking for help when you have so much trouble of your own."

Mama seemed to shrink. "Everyone has trouble. What can we do for you, Molly?"

"Well, Peter is a strong boy for his age, but the herd has been running wild all summer. I'm afraid an eight-year-old is just not up to some of those unbroken yearlings."

Joel sat in the gathering room, listening. "I'll bring the herd in for you, ma'am," he offered, setting down his newspaper.

Relief loosened the woman's smile. "I'll pay you a dollar."

"There's no need for that. Be glad to."

"Nonsense. I need the work done, and if I'm to drag you away from your own chores, I insist that you take it."

"We accept gratefully," Mama put in. "Thank you, Molly. You're sure you won't stay for tea?"

"I can't. I have to finish a new shirt for Peter. It's astonishing how quickly one boy grows."

"Say hello to him for me," Justin called.

Mrs. Patton waved in reply as she stepped outside. "Oh, I almost forgot!" she exclaimed, rummaging in her apron pocket. "I picked up this letter for you at the post office this afternoon."

Mama's fingers trembled as she reached for it. Joel closed the door as Mama sank into her rocking chair. Hannah and Justin gathered around.

Joel took the letter and opened it, reading in a low voice.

September 19, 1862
My beloved family,

By the time you read this, news will have reached you of South Mountain and Antietam. I posted this as soon as possible to relieve your concerns. By the grace of God, I am whole and Seth is well. How I wish I could say as much for the rest of my company. We have lost so many!

My heart is especially heavy for our dear daughter. You can tell her that Tommy fought bravely, and that he died a hero,

79

helping a comrade off the field. And let her know her letter arrived in time. For one night, Tommy was the proudest papa you could ever imagine. He is sorely missed.

A sob interrupted Joel's reading, and the flash of Maddy's yellow dressing gown disappeared around the stairway wall. For ten days, ever since Tommy's memorial service, she had taken to her bed. Mama brought up meals that remained mostly untouched, and Hannah had begun sleeping on the sofa so she wouldn't be wakened by her sister's wracking sobs in the middle of the night.

Tommy's death had left Hannah deeply saddened. She had always liked Tommy, and she regretted that he'd only been in the family a short time. But when the immediate shock of his passing wore off, life went on for her as it always did. She even harbored a secret relief that it was neither Seth nor Pa who had died.

Mama sighed, deep and broken. "Keep reading, Joel. I'll tend her when you've finished."

I will spare you further details of the battlefield. Let it suffice to say that war is a horror God never intended his creation to suffer. But it is also a crucible that shows each man the purity or contamination of his own character. The 17th Michigan has done itself proud. Our boys stood firm as granite, even in the face of death. There are some who have taken to calling us "The Stonewall Regiment" because we could not be moved.

We are holed up for the time being, licking our wounds. McClellan has not pursued Lee, a choice for which he is taking heat from some individuals. He has made mistakes, but I would not want to fill his shoes, so I will remain silent.

Your letters conjure up familiar visions that sustain me through my worst moments. I am pleased to hear that home, at least, has known peace and prosperity. I know it must be difficult with Seth and me gone, but I am confident you will manage just fine. I am so proud of your hard work. I miss you all terribly and long for the day I can set foot again on my own little piece of the earth.

> *With all my love,*
> *Henry Stanton Wallace*

Seth had enclosed a letter in the same envelope. Joel read:

September 20, 1862
Dear Mama and everybody,

I am so angry and frustrated I could scream! It is no wonder this war has lasted so long. The Union army is commanded by idiots. General McClellan, especially, is an incompetent nincompoop. I found out he had Lee's battle plan in his hand. By some miraculous chance, Lee mislaid it and it was picked up by some of our boys. McClellan could have pounded him! But as usual he took a day and a half to act, and our chance was lost. By the time we received marching orders, Lee had plugged up the passes through the Blue Ridge and we had to fight our way through South Mountain where we lost many men.

Then, when both armies gathered at Sharpsburg, McClellan further proved his ineptitude. We vastly outnumbered Lee, but McClellan failed to make a coordinated assault. Besides that, he held back a quarter of the army. They didn't even fight! Had that featherhead poured on all our strength in a united attack, Lee would have had to surrender. He was backed up against the Potomac River with nowhere to go.

Our own corps commander, General Burnside, is no less a fool. He spent hours throwing our boys at a bridge over Antietam Creek when we could have waded the blasted thing only a few yards away, out of enemy fire. It was useless slaughter and it stalled our corps for hours when we might have aided the attack.

Thousands and thousands of good boys fell at Antietam. You could never imagine the number, Mama. They were tumbled over each other in piles, North and South together. And for what? They tell me we won a victory. But we could have ended the war.

I tell you, if a bullet doesn't get me first, I'm going to die of frustration and anger.

> *Your affectionate son,*
> *Seth Wallace*

Seth's reckless energy transferred to Hannah as she listened to his account. The same blood flowed through her veins, the same fire. With Tommy's passing the battlefield lost some of its luster, but she still yearned for the adventure her brother was living. She was the daughter of pioneers! Would she always be stuck in this stale corner of the Union? She scowled out at the growing darkness, chafing at her own dumb luck.

The evening was warm, and night sounds floated in the open window: crickets and cicadas and tree frogs by the hundreds. The trees had begun dropping their leaves, and October would soon usher in frost. Even now a cool breeze gusted into the gathering room. Hannah reached to shut the window, and the breeze whisked her hair back from her face. She paused, an idea taking root in her mind.

She couldn't join Seth, but maybe Wayland still held an adventure or two.

***

The next morning Hannah made another delivery of eggs to Mr. Lawson. But this time she snuck away without changing into her dress. And before leaving, she filled her pockets with corn and tied Seth's oldest straw hat on her head.

Mr. Lawson looked up in surprise, taking in her unusual appearance. "Is this how your mother is dressing you now?"

She grinned. "Don't tell her. She'd take a switch to me."

"I see. Well, it is sensible, I suppose." His voice dropped to a whisper. "And the hat is much better than some of Mrs. Clark's creations."

Hannah giggled and handed Mr. Lawson the eggs. "Mama wants to put the money on our bill."

"That would be fine." He made the tabulation and handed the basket back.

"Can I leave that here for now? I'll pick it up later."

He shrugged and tucked it behind the counter. "All right with me."

"Thanks. See you later."

"'Bye, Hannah. Tell your mother I'll be over this afternoon to speak with her."

"I will!"

She crossed quickly to the post office. "Hello, Mr. Briggs. Got a letter here for Pa."

"Good morning, Hannah." The postman hopped off his stool and added the envelope to a stack of outgoing mail. "That was a mighty speedy reply. I hope it doesn't mean your menfolk aren't well," he prompted.

"They're both fine. You know Pa. He'd find something good to say even if the sun went dark. But Seth is shooting enough sparks to set the whole army ablaze. They ought to make him general."

As she spoke, Hannah heard the dull rattle of many hooves approaching. Mr. Briggs consulted his pocket watch. "Morning stage, two minutes early."

Moments later, the vehicle pulled up in front of the Wayland House where Hannah could see it through the window. Several passengers alighted and entered the hotel, but one gentleman in a top hat sought out the driver and berated him heartily. The driver let him wind down then simply pointed toward the toll booth.

83

"Seth's finger doesn't bother him much?" Mr. Briggs fished, eager for details.

"Doesn't seem to. His writing reads fine anyway."

"Well, I'm glad to hear it. Folks have been asking about him, you know."

"I'm sure they have."

She turned to leave, but the gentleman from the stage had reached the booth and rapped sharply on the window. Mr. Briggs slid it open. "Good morning, sir. How may I help you?"

The man had heavy brows that puckered in an ill-tempered frown. His clothes appeared fashionable and well-tailored, but at close range Hannah could see his top hat looked rather mashed.

"You can tell your company this road is abominable," the man complained. "When I set out from Plainwell this morning, this hat was new."

"I do apologize," Mr. Briggs said hastily. "I've hit my head myself a time or—"

"And," the man continued, sweeping his headwear away to reveal a shiny bald scalp, "I had hair!"

Hannah clapped a hand over her mouth and left Mr. Briggs to his dilemma.

A mile north of the crossroads, the Rabbit River arced around town like rope hung over a nail. Hannah jogged up the Plank Road past the tannery to where the river flowed through a broad, stumpy meadow. She and Wes sometimes came here to fish, and almost every time, the Patton's herd of quarter horses made an appearance to graze on the sweet grass.

She sat down to wait on one of the stumps in the middle of the field where she could catch the sun's weak, early rays when it peeked from behind the clouds. The grass was cold and wet on her bare feet. She shivered and tucked them underneath her.

She didn't have long to wait. Within the hour, pounding hooves echoed through the woods and all seven of Mr. Patton's remaining animals pranced out into the field, the youngest ones kicking up their heels in a wild display of energy. One of the mares lowered its head to graze, and eventually the others followed her example.

Hannah left her rock and slowly approached them. A few of the closer horses pricked up their ears and looked at her, but most paid her little mind. She picked out the one she knew to be the fastest—a three-year-old stallion with a white blaze down its nose—and pulled a handful of grain from her pockets.

The rattle and smell of corn drew inquisitive glances all around, but only the stallion plodded nearer, stretching out its neck and blowing moist heat onto Hannah's hand. She emptied her pockets and poured the grain into a pile on the ground. The horse plunged its muzzle in, and while it was distracted, she leaped onto its back.

The stallion snorted with surprise. Five months had passed since it carried a rider. It flung up its legs and tossed its head, but Hannah stuck like a flea on a dog, squeezing her knees and knotting her fingers in the long mane. The stallion plunged back to earth, bolting as soon as its feet touched the ground.

Instantly the world blurred. Hannah could hardly draw breath against the wind that pressed her face. Even on Rounder she had never known such speed. She thrilled with the hot power beneath her and with the sheer, wild danger as the stallion sprinted across the meadow. She felt completely free. Free from the suffocating crowd of her siblings, free from the pressure of living up to her brothers, free from the life of work and boredom she was bound to.

After a minute or two the stallion's reckless pace fell off, but it continued running with smooth, powerful strides that ate up the ground. A glance behind showed the whole herd plunging along in their wake, following their leader like dutiful soldiers.

After three easy miles, the Lumberton mill came into view. Hannah snatched the hat off her head and waved it beside the stallion's head to turn it. With another burst of speed, it swerved onto the old Indian trail that had been so important before the Plank Road went through. She let the stallion choose its pace, using her hat again only to guide it onto the wagon track that led past the Wallace farm and on to the Pattons'.

Breaking out of the woods, she nearly ran over Mr. Covington who had set up his easel at the edge of the field. She whooped the stallion back up to full speed, laughing as the startled man stumbled out of the way with his paints spilling and his canvas toppling.

An easy canter brought them to the Patton pasture. Hannah guided the stallion through the gate and rolled off its back, fastening the barrier behind the last horse. The herd circled twice, manes tossing and tails streaming proudly. Their nostrils flared and their sleek sides heaved as they sucked in breath, but within minutes their breathing regulated and they fell again to grazing.

Mrs. Patton stopped by at lunchtime to drop off the dollar. "Joel was so prompt," she complimented, "and he didn't even stay to collect his pay."

When the door closed behind her, Mama turned puzzled eyes on Joel. "I thought you and Justin brought the pumpkins into town today. Whenever did you find time?"

Joel started to speak when Hannah's wide grin caught his eye. Her secret passed between them. He winked—a barely perceptible flutter of his eyelashes—and answered Mama with a careless shrug.

***

That evening, Mr. Lawson appeared at the door with his hat held in his big hands. "Good evening, Mrs. Wallace. I was wondering if I could speak with you a moment?"

"Of course, Mr. Lawson. Do come in." She held the door wide and the shopkeeper stood looking about uncertainly. "Can I offer you a bite of supper? We're just about to sit down."

"That'd be mighty fine," he answered with an appreciative smile. "I get right tired of my own cooking."

Justin piped up from his seat at the table, "You oughta get married so your wife can cook for you. How come you never did?"

Hannah set a platter of flapjacks on the table and cuffed him on the back of the head. "Women can do more than cook."

"Justin, Hannah, that's enough. Let's sit down. Mr. Lawson, you may take Henry's seat at the head of the table."

"Mama, I don't think I could keep a thing down tonight." Maddy rubbed her belly, but the look of distrust she aimed at the shopkeeper betrayed her real reasons for fleeing. Mama let her go without an argument.

After grace, the shopkeeper savored a syrup-soaked bite. "Mmm. Hannah, you're right, of course, but if I happened on a woman that cooked like your mama, I confess I just might take the plunge."

Justin gave Hannah a smug look, and she pulled a face in his direction. "I'm never getting married," she announced.

Mama looked up in surprise. "Hannah, what a thing to say! Why on earth not?"

"I don't want to waste my life slaving for everybody else."

Mama smiled. "You're young yet. You'll change your mind. There's pleasure in bringing up a family."

87

But Hannah shook her head stubbornly. "Not me. I have too many things to do."

"Like what?" Mr. Lawson encouraged.

"I'm going to climb a mountain," she told him. "And I'm going to visit the president. And I'm going to cross the ocean on a giant ship and tour Europe. Maybe I'll even go to Africa."

"Mercy!" Mama exclaimed.

Joel offered her the ghost of a smile. "Then you better marry a rich man. We don't have money like that."

"I just told you, I'm not getting married!"

"Good thing," Justin jeered, "'cause there isn't a boy alive who would marry you anyway!"

"Actually, you've touched on the reason for my visit," Mr. Lawson put in.

Justin's face opened in shock. "You want to marry Hannah?"

A laugh like the throb of an engine boomed out of the big man. "No, no. I'm afraid I'd be an old man by the time she changed her mind. No, Joel touched on the reason I've come." He turned to Mama. "It is no secret that hailstorm destroyed a good share of your wheat crop."

Mama's eyes slid to her plate and she nodded.

"It has also come to my attention that your bank note is due very soon, and you are unable to meet it."

Mama stared up at him. "Now how do you know that?"

Lawson smiled sympathetically. "Joel has been all over town feeling out buyers for certain items, including your north pasture. It was not hard to figure out."

Mama sighed. "Josiah Patton has always wanted that bit of land, but with him gone to war and their herd of horses so depleted, Molly just couldn't commit to the sale. Joel was trying to find another buyer."

"Do you have much time left?"

Mama shook her head. "I'm afraid not. Oh, I hate the thought of the bank getting what we have worked so hard for!"

"I'd hate to see that as well. Mrs. Wallace, what if I told you that I have enough capital to offer you a small loan, say till the end of the year? Would that be of help?"

Mama gasped. "Oh, Mr. Lawson, truly? But you've already extended so much credit to others. Are you sure it's wise?"

Mr. Lawson chuckled. "Don't worry about me, Mrs. Wallace. They are secure investments. Would you be interested?"

Mama beamed at him. "Mr. Lawson, you are an angel!"

Chapter Ten

Hannah always thought of autumn as a calm valley between two stormy mountains. The harvest, that insanely busy period of gathering and storing away food, was finished and cold weather would soon usher in a whole new host of chores. But for a few weeks the beauty of fall foliage and cool temperatures drove her into the woods.

There she might watch the chipmunks bicker and scamper through dry leaves with their mouths stuffed full of nuts. Or chuckle at the fat, rolling bodies of skunks and groundhogs as they browsed for just one more mouthful before their winter sleep. Regretfully, school always interrupted those sweet, lingering days.

Hannah walked to town alone. Justin had run halfway to the schoolhouse already, eager to reunite with his friends. She could just see his blond head bobbing over the farthest hill. Usually Joel accompanied them, but with Pa gone, Joel's school days were probably over.

A crowd of noisy children chased each other through the schoolyard like a colony of squirrels. Off to one side, three ingenious little girls had tied together lengths of twine and weighted them with an old spool. Now they were busily swinging their jump rope over a bare spot in the yard and chanting silly rhymes with the fervor of a camp preacher. Wes, however, was nowhere in sight.

Sue Ellen waited primly on the schoolhouse steps with Mary Burns, playing a game of cat's cradle. "Hannah!" she welcomed. "Come join us. If you can get your fingers in here, you can take my place. I've gone several rounds already."

The girls' fingers were woven with string like miniature looms.

"No thanks. Have you seen Wes?"

The design tangled and the two girls shook their hands loose.

"He's out back," Sue Ellen told her. "I think he's in trouble."

Depositing her books on the steps, Hannah went looking and found her friend stacking firewood behind the schoolhouse with less than his usual enthusiasm. Crossing her arms, she leaned casually against the corner of the school. "Are you wooing Miss West or just getting an early start working off your bad grades?"

Wes tossed a slab onto the pile and scowled. "Hannah, never let your pa catch you sneaking a draw on his pipe."

Hannah's laughter rang out above the sound of children playing. "Was it worth it?"

Wes shuddered. "He made me smoke the whole confounded thing. Got so sick I crawled behind the stable and puked out my socks. Now I have to stay before and after school until this whole load is stacked."

Her eyes sparkled. "Maybe I can get Pa to send home some good Virginia tobacco for your next birthday."

He shot her a look of pure disgust.

She chuckled. "Say, were you here when Tommy volunteered to stack wood for Mrs. Clark?" As the memory stirred, hoots of laughter began to bubble out of her till she

91

could hardly stand up.

Wes rested against the pile and shook his head. "I never had to sit under the old biddy."

She gasped for breath. "He filled the quills of five feathers with gunpowder and smuggled them to school in the center of a half-rotten log. Then he stacked a nice pile for her, put his piece on top, and just waited. Old Lady Clark threw it in the stove after lunch. It took about ten minutes to burn down to the powder, but when it started popping you should have seen her dance!" she whooped.

Wes slapped his leg and howled, but Hannah's joy in telling the story suddenly spluttered like a spent candle. Somehow, the memory made Tommy's loss more real.

"He got expelled for two weeks," she finished lamely.

Wes scooched up next to her and punched her gently on the shoulder. "It's too bad about Tommy. A real hard knock. But you can't let it get you down. He died on his own terms, for the good of the country and for the glory of the North."

Her guts felt like cold mashed potatoes, and for a moment she wondered if glory was enough to trade a life for.

"Just think of how he lived!" Wes continued. "Jiminy! Traveling across the country, seeing new cities, sleeping in a tent, camping with his buddies, cooking over an open fire then singing songs and telling stories around it after dark."

The pictures Wes painted began to whet her old appetite.

"And when duty called, he met it. He fought bravely and died valiantly. He's a hero, Hannah!"

Yes, Tommy had lived before he died. The freedom, the excitement, the expectation... She knew if the opportunity arose for her to escape the drudgery of her life, she would take it, too. Even at such a risk.

Her good humor flickered back. "I believe you have a job to finish, General McClellan."

Wes snapped a sharp salute. "Aye, aye, General Grant!"

With renewed gusto, he threw four more logs on the pile before Miss West rang the school bell.

The teacher couldn't have been any older than Seth. She was pretty, with dark curls gathered at her neck. She beamed at them from the front of the room and a dimple appeared in one cheek. "Good morning, class."

"Good morning, Miss West," they chanted.

"Welcome to a new school year. I am pleased to see all of you. Let's begin this morning by taking roll."

As the teacher called out names and jotted down attendance, Hannah reacquainted herself with the schoolroom. The same painted blackboard stretched across the front of the room. The same pictures of Lincoln and Washington graced the walls. Maps of Michigan and America hung in their same places, and the cloakroom held the same lunch pails. The only difference from last year was a few new faces and the absence of others.

Miss West folded the roll book. After prayer and the pledge of allegiance, she stood before the class and smiled. "Much has happened since the last time we gathered. Does anyone have anything to share?"

A little boy in the front row slipped his hand up. "My dog had puppies, Miss West. Five black ones and a golden. They're four weeks old now."

"How wonderful, Samuel!" the teacher exclaimed. "Have you named them?"

"Just the one we're going to keep. Pa says it's foolish to name animals we ain't keepin—"

"Aren't keeping."

"—but I came up with names for all of them and didn't tell him."

"I would like to hear about them. Will you make your puppies the subject of our first composition?"

93

The little boy nodded his head seriously, and Miss West called on one of the older boys. "James."

James Beasley stood up with a half-smirk. Everyone knew he was sweet on the teacher, and he sometimes caused a ruckus just for the attention. He sauntered to the front of the room and cleared his throat with mock importance. "The Carter barn burned down in August," he announced.

Loud guffaws sounded from his friends in the back of the room. "Shoot, everyone knows that!" one of them burst out. Candles, lanterns, and fireplaces could start a blaze that quickly turned deadly. It was a fear everyone lived with, but the Carter barn was old news.

Miss West warned the boys with a stern look before addressing James. "I did hear about that. I assume everyone got out safely?"

"They just lost some equipment," James told her. "The stock was all outside, and it didn't spread to the house. New barn's already up."

Half of the town had turned out to help rebuild, and judging from the snickers coming from the back row, most of James's friends had been there too. But they didn't call out again.

"I'm glad it wasn't worse. Thank you, James, for that update."

James grinned widely as he rejoined his friends and took their ribbing.

"Anyone else?" She scanned the silent room. "Nobody? Then let's start out with current events. Can anyone name the policy change Mr. Lincoln made just a few weeks ago?"

Several students raised their hands. The Emancipation Proclamation was still popping hot news. The farmers lounging near the fireplace in the Wayland House rehashed it every evening, and it was still the topic of choice in the schoolyard after church.

94

Miss West called on Wes.

"He freed the slaves, ma'am." Wes grinned smartly, winking at Hannah. Hannah rolled her eyes.

"That's right, Wesley. Which ones did he free?"

Wes froze. "All of them?"

"I'm sorry, that's incorrect."

Hannah leered at her friend as he slumped in his seat.

Across the aisle Sue Ellen raised her hand. "He only freed the slaves in rebel states that haven't returned to the Union by January first. So technically, it hasn't taken effect yet."

Hannah and Wes exchanged glances and rolled their eyes.

"Very good, Sue Ellen. Did anyone else read the copy of the Proclamation printed in the *Record*?"

A few hands went up. George Stockdale called out with the same bravado his brother Tommy had always showed, "My daddy read it to us and cursed Mr. Lincoln after every other line." That made the boys in the back of the room laugh again.

"George, you may stand in the corner, please."

George shrugged and stood up, towering over the teacher on his way to the front. "Sorry, Miss West."

Wes waggled his hand. "What good will the Proclamation do, really? No one in the South is going to listen to him."

"That's a good point, Wesley. It probably won't have a sweeping effect, but it will cause some changes to be made. At the turn of the year, it will be illegal for escaped slaves to be captured and returned to their owners, so bounty hunters will be put out of business. In addition, slaves will be set free in sections of the South that are liberated by the army. Before, we were fighting just to preserve the Union. Now, in addition, we are fighting to free the slaves, and not everyone agrees with it," she said, glancing at George.

95

"I agree with it, Miss West," Sue Ellen stated. "I think it's wrong for anyone to own another person."

"She would," Hannah whispered to Wes.

"Hannah," Miss West intoned, coming to stand meaningfully beside her seat, "perhaps you'd like to share your views."

"No, thank you, Miss West."

"Really, Hannah. I'd like to hear what you think about the president's law."

Hannah glanced at Sue Ellen, then at George listening from the corner. She shrugged. "I don't really care one way or the other."

"So you don't believe slavery is wrong?"

The teacher waited, expecting her to continue. Hannah took a breath. "I guess I don't hold too much sympathy for slaves. Sure they have to work. So do I. My family works hard for what we have. And if we don't work, we don't eat. At least slaves have someone giving them food and shelter and clothing at the end of the day."

"Well spoken, Hannah," Miss West praised, "but you have overlooked some important differences. For example, you benefit directly from your work. Unlike a slave, no one else can claim your profit. You also have legal rights: of land ownership, due process, the right to bring suit, and many others. As a free person, you never have to suffer mistreatment at the hands of an owner."

Hannah shrugged again. The law meant nothing to her. She'd never even seen a Negro, slave or free.

The day passed slowly. By afternoon, Hannah's seat ached, her head ached, and her hand ached. It required all her willpower to stay in her chair. Even so, she fidgeted like the little boys in the front row. When Miss West finally rang the bell, she dashed down the aisle ahead of everyone.

Justin exploded out the door behind her with his slingshot in his hand. Hannah caught his arm. "Justin, tell

Mama I'll be a little late for chores."

"Why?" His chin thrust out.

"Because there's something I have to do."

He narrowed his eyes. "You don't have nuthin' to do. You're just shirking again."

Hannah's voice tightened. "Shut up, Justin."

"I don't have to. You think you can do whatever you want, just because you're older. But you sure ain't good for much of anything."

"Shut up, Justin!"

But he was unstoppable. "You're just sneaking off with Wes again. Probably end up like Maddy. In fact, I wish you would get yourself hitched and move off somewhere."

"I'm nothing like Maddy!" Hannah grabbed him by the ear. "Take it back, Justin!"

"All right! All right!" he winced, balancing on tiptoe.

She thrust him away and he rubbed at the sore spot. "But I'm gonna tell Mama you're shirking your chores!" he hollered, setting off at a run.

Hannah waited till he was well down the Plank Road before storming off in the other direction.

Mrs. Clark answered her knock. "He's out back." She jerked her head to the rear and shut the door. Hannah stomped around the house and found the artist detailing the sketch of a hand. He looked up and appraised her. "What's the matter with you? You look mad enough to horsewhip your grandmother."

"Never met her, but my brother would do."

"Ah, sibling rivalry. Makes me glad I never had children."

"There's no rivalry," she scowled. "No matter what he says, I can outrun, outwork, and outshoot him, hands down. I'm worth two of him any day! I'm more than equal to any son Pa ever had."

Mr. Covington scratched absently at his chin. "In my

experience," he drawled, "it's the fellow who knows he's guilty that always proclaims his innocence the loudest."

"What do you mean, guilty?" Hannah could feel her anger burning her face. "Are you taking his side? Just because women can't go to war or—or vote, you think all they're good for is to mind the house, mind the farm, and mind the children?" She glared at him. "If anyone's guilty, it's the men who try to hold women back."

Mr. Covington gave her a keen glance. "All I'm saying is that you must be pretty convinced of your brother's words or you wouldn't try so hard to prove them wrong."

Hannah's mouth popped open then snapped shut with a click.

"Anyway, he's got you so red in the face folks will think I'm painting an Indian. Go get a drink of water and calm yourself down or we'll end this session right now."

Hannah wanted nothing more. Her pulse raced like a runaway horse, and sweat oozed from her whole body. At that moment, there was no one she hated more in the entire world than Elijah P. Covington. But she remembered the money in his pockets and stalked to the well to throw down the bucket.

How could he say those things? Of course she wasn't trying to prove anything. At least, she wasn't trying to prove herself to Justin. She already knew she could best him.

Then why did her brother rankle her so badly? She didn't care what he thought. She only cared what Pa thought. She wanted Pa to be as proud of her as he was of any son—Justin, Joel, or Jeremy.

Jeremy!

She jolted to a stop. She wasn't trying to best Justin. She was trying to best Jeremy!

Hannah plunked to her knees. She could see it now. For years she'd been trying to take the place of that baby. How could she possibly live up to such an impossible goal?

No wonder she hated the farm.

But what could she do? She had to make up for Jeremy. Pa was counting on her, and she simply wouldn't allow herself to disappoint him.

She returned ten minutes later and thoughtfully took up her position.

"Hold steady right there," the artist told her. "I've got to start over. Some wild fool galloped a herd of horses over me the other day, and I spilled paint all over the canvas. Dad gum hooligan," he muttered.

Despite herself, Hannah felt laughter kicking up its heels like one of Mrs. Patton's quarter horses, and she fought to tame it. Mr. Covington griped behind his canvas, but she didn't care. It served the old buzzard right.

Her face must have registered better spirits, because Mr. Covington worked steadily. When he spoke again, his question took Hannah off guard. "Seems you're a girl who knows her mind. So, if it isn't bent toward housework or farm work, what exactly is it bent toward?"

Hannah blinked and collected her thoughts. What did she want, really?

In a household of so many people, she hoped to establish her own identity. She was tired of being lumped in with her sister. She didn't want to become her mother. And she had no desire to live up to whatever her dead brother might have become. She wanted to be herself, to live out the fire of her own spirit.

She answered carefully, "I guess I need to figure out who I am. I don't want to wake up someday to find that every dream, every adventure, every hope of proving myself has passed me by and that I've become an old woman beaten into something everyone else has made me."

Mr. Covington thought on that awhile, chewing his bottom lip. "And just how are you planning to work that out?"

"I don't know yet," she admitted, staring at that unknown place where the sky kissed the land. "But someday I will. Someday I'm leaving."

Chapter Eleven

"Hannah, will you bring this package to Mr. Blankford? His son was badly wounded at Antietam, and he's going down to visit the hospital. He offered to deliver it to your father for us."

Mama had been busy for many evenings knitting warm socks, mufflers, and mittens for her soldiers. Today she packed them all into a pasteboard box along with a dozen apples and Pa's favorite kind of cookies. "They might grow stale," she admitted, "but they'll be a sight better than beans and hardtack."

The afternoon was mild so Hannah left Rounder home, navigating the planks to town with her own bare feet.

She liked Mr. Blankford. He was a pudgy, jolly fellow, a little older than Pa, with spreading laugh lines etched into the skin around his eyes. But today, as he opened the door, he looked more thoughtful than merry.

Hannah presented her package. "Mama said to tell you thank you very, very much."

The lines deepened and he almost smiled, but not quite. "You tell her she's very, very welcome. I'll do my best to put it directly into Henry's hands."

"What if you can't find him?" she asked. "What if his company is gone?"

"Then I'll find out where and rustle up someone who can get it where it needs to go. Don't worry, young lady. Your Pa will get it."

She turned to go, then whirled impulsively and threw her arms around the man, planting a kiss on his weathered cheek. "Give him that for me too, would you?"

He did chuckle then. "That might carry more weight coming from you, but I'll do my best."

"Thank you, Mr. Blankford. I hope your son is all right."

"Me too, lass."

She moved quickly through town and was watching Mr. Lawson's big tomcat dart around the corner of the Wayland House when Wes flagged her down from the long front porch. "Hannah!" Beside him stood his brother, home from the war, looking strong and recovered from his injury.

"Marcus!" she exclaimed, rushing to greet him. But as she drew near, she could see he didn't return her enthusiasm. In fact, he little resembled the carefree young man she remembered. His face looked thin, and his skin stretched over it like a tarp tightened down over a loaded wagon.

"Marcus, how good to see you! You look wonderful."

She faltered over that last word just a bit as the warm brown eyes that once sparkled with humor glowered down at her.

When he didn't reply, she stumbled on. "I mean, you could use a few good meals. Seth says army food isn't fit to choke a hog. But, really, you look fantastic! When Wes told me you'd been injured I thought—" She stopped in confusion, then shrugged. "It's just good to see you home."

Marcus turned slightly, and Hannah's eyes landed on an empty sleeve pinned up to his elbow. Her smile crumbled.

102

"Still look fantastic?" he asked bitterly.

"Oh, Marcus!" she whispered.

Wes cut in. "I told him he should be proud of it. I would be."

Marcus gave them a cynical smile. "It's a matter of great pride when a man can no longer work. When he can't even support himself, let alone a family. But then, what woman would want a one-armed man anyway?"

Hannah didn't know what to say. Any response would seem flimsy and trite and entirely worthless in the face of such deep hurt.

Marcus laughed bitterly. "I'll be twenty years old next month. I have a whole lifetime to be proud."

He turned away and disappeared inside the hotel.

Hannah jabbed Wes hard with her elbow. "You never told me he lost his arm!" she hissed.

"I didn't know! Marcus didn't say anything in his letter. Just that he'd been injured."

"And you couldn't guess when he wrote with his left hand?" Her voice dripped sarcasm.

"Someone else wrote the letter," he snapped. "Don't take it out on me. I'm not the one who lopped off his arm."

She sighed. "I'm sorry. It's just so sad. How did your parents take it?"

"How do you think? They're just glad to have him home. Pa didn't even say told-you-so. Mama's a little worried about him, though."

"She should be. He seems so depressed."

"He'll be fine," Wes reassured her. "He can do lots of stuff one-handed. Like run a hotel, or work in a bank, or do any number of desk jobs."

"I suppose you're right. He'll learn to live with it."

"You bet he will!" Wes grinned. "I can't wait till he shakes off this funk and tells us how he lost it." He pulled his arm inside his shirt and let his sleeve hang empty. "Golly! I bet it's a good story."

Hannah stared at him incredulously. "I've got to go home." Her words were thick with disgust.

"Right. See you tomorrow." He jerked his sleeve to make it wave at her.

She ran over the planks, the sight of that flapping sleeve etched in her memory. But when she tried to recall the lean, bitter face of Marcus, she saw only the features of her father.

***

The morning was cold, with frost still lingering in the hollows. It was the kind of dawn that asked for a hot bowl of oatmeal with a touch of maple syrup, but Hannah's breakfast would have to wait a little longer.

"I need you to leach the ashes today," her mother had said as soon as Hannah bounced down the stairs. "There's hot water on the stove."

Autumn chores had begun. There would be no school for many days.

Maddy had reemerged to join their labors, but she was gaunt and listless, hardly the same person she once was. She worked steadily and silently, like a wooden puppet, showing no emotion at all. And she never mentioned her husband's name. When Hannah had to be with her, she stepped carefully, as if tiptoeing through a litter of new piglets.

Hannah carried the water out to the shed. In the corner, several barrels held ashes that had been collected from cook fires all year long. There was also a wooden hopper that looked like a smaller barrel on legs, except the bottom was made out of thin slats.

Hannah covered the slats with a foot of straw and then filled the hopper with ashes. Placing an empty bucket under it, she poured hot water over the top. Soon a foul-smelling stream of brown liquid flowed through the slats and trickled into the bucket below.

Hannah would have to perform the task several more times before she had leached enough of the strong brown lye to make soap. And soap was just the beginning. Firewood had to be chopped and stacked, and insulation piled around the base of the house and the barn. No doubt the boys would round up the hogs today. Now that it was cold enough to preserve the meat, the animals must be slaughtered, salted, and smoked.

Slaughtering day also meant making sausage and cracklings. Some of the fat would be rendered into candles. The rest would be combined with the brown lye and boiled to make soap.

Leaving the hopper to drain, Hannah went in to breakfast. Justin followed her, toting a pail brimming with milk. They sat down just as Mama spooned cornmeal mush into five bowls.

Joel shuffled through a library of papers spread out in front of him. "I sold the last of the potatoes and pumpkins. We haven't purchased anything for weeks. The butter and egg money has paid off our store credit, and we should get a fair price for the hogs. I think we could pay off Lawson on time if taxes weren't due."

Mama closed her eyes wearily. Suddenly, she slammed the spoon onto the table, gouging a chunk out of the wood. "Blast this war! And blast Mr. Lincoln! He pays your pa for soldiering then demands it right back again in taxes. How on earth is anyone supposed to get ahead?"

She kneaded her forehead with one hand. "At least when you don't make much, they can't take much away."

Hannah listened soberly. Perhaps this would be a good time to share her secret. Excusing herself from the table and scrambling upstairs to her room, she rummaged in her sock drawer and pulled out the money she had been saving from

Mr. Covington. Over the past six weeks, she had made almost four dollars. She knew it wasn't much, but maybe it would boost Mama's spirits.

Scampering down the steps, she dropped the money on the table in front of Mama with a loud clatter. Four bodies went motionless, and four pairs of eyes focused on the shiny coins. Hannah wished Mr. Covington could paint the look on Justin's face.

"Mercy, child!" Mama exclaimed. "Wherever did you get that?"

Hannah smirked triumphantly at her little brother. "I've been modeling for Mr. Covington's paintings. He pays me each time we finish."

"You've been what?" Mama exclaimed.

"It's fine, Mama. Mrs. Carver knows, and Mrs. Clark has chaperoned every session. I wanted to surprise you."

Mama closed her eyes again. "Bless you, child. Joel, put this with the rest. We'll pay Uncle Sam first. Lawson has promised an extension. At any rate, I'd rather have Mr. Lawson acquire our farm than the government."

***

Everything gave way for the flurry of work except church services and sessions with Mr. Covington. Even when the kitchen was full of raw pork, Mama sent Hannah for the scheduled hour, calling in Justin to take her place.

"But Mama, making sausage is women's work," her brother groused.

"Hush," Mama ordered, up to her elbows in grease. "It's the work of anyone who wants to eat this winter. Now grind."

A chill wind gusted and the sky threatened to spill over. Whether it would pour forth rain or snow was anyone's guess. Hannah wrapped up snug in a muffler and an extra shawl and welcomed Rounder's warmth beneath her. As she rode past the smokehouse and out of the yard, the sharp smell of burning hickory chips tickled her nostrils.

Mr. Covington had commandeered a corner of Mrs. Clark's parlor during Hannah's last visit.

"You absolutely will not!" the old woman had declared as they carried canvas and paints in from the chilly backyard. "Take it upstairs this instant!"

"Now woman, you know my window faces north," he snapped. "There's not enough light up there to fasten my bowtie. How am I supposed to paint?"

"I don't give two flips of a lamb's tail how you do it, as long as the mess isn't in my good sitting room. What will my other boarders say?"

"I'm your only boarder!" Mr. Covington roared. "There isn't another man on God's green earth fool enough to rent from you!"

In the end, the artist agreed to pay an additional fifty cents a week for the use of the sunny parlor, and Mrs. Clark left them alone, happily clutching her hard currency.

Hannah entered the room, which was strewn with pictures like the bedroom upstairs. She gasped as she caught sight of herself standing in a barnyard, clutching a milk pail in front of her and staring wistfully into the distance. Mr. Covington had finished the painting several sessions ago, but she hadn't bothered to look. Now she studied the fine details, the colors and shadows and lines that replicated her face exactly.

Then a second painting grabbed her eye. She picked it up and studied a band of quarter horses with heads raised and tails streaming, galloping freely across a field strewn with autumn leaves. On the lead stallion perched a small figure with faded trousers, windblown hair, and an expression of pure joy. That face, too, she was astonished to see, exactly matched her own!

So Mr. Covington had known who ruined his first painting and nearly ran him into the ground. Yet he never uttered one word.

The artist strode into the room as she clutched the canvas. "It's very good," she muttered, feeling foolish. Why must her face always burn so?

She dropped the painting and squared her shoulders to face him. "No, it's beautiful. The light on the trees, the wind, the color, the fluid movements. It's like the horses are really there, running across the canvas."

Mr. Covington arched one heavy brow. "I believe when you signed on we agreed that I needed no critic, young lady." But Hannah thought she spotted just a hint of satisfaction in the curl of his lip.

He positioned her in a new pose, sitting with a sunhat dangling from one hand and a rake leaning across her lap, as if resting from a garden chore. The time off her feet was welcome, almost restful, and she used the quiet hour to brood over her father.

She missed him terribly. No letters had arrived from either Pa or Seth for nearly three weeks, not since the letter from Antietam. Had Mama's package reached Pa yet? Would Mr. Blankford be able to find him? Perhaps he and Seth had moved on already. Perhaps there had been more fighting. Perhaps—but she wouldn't even let her thoughts drift in that direction.

She never worried much about Seth. He was the one with the injury, and she knew the risk of infection was high, but Seth would be fine. Seth was always fine.

She remembered two years ago, when the whole family caught influenza. The weather had grown bitter, and illness had swept through the house till everyone was down with it. Everyone except Seth. Pa was the worst of them all. He was nearly delirious, but he kept choring, kindly and foolishly taking on too much work till he fell unconscious. Ma had sent for Doctor Graves, who diagnosed pneumonia and ordered Pa to stay warm, dry, and quiet for several weeks.

It ate Pa up something fierce having to stay inside helpless while others took over his work. But Seth bore up well. He took Pa's place like a man, though he was only sixteen at the time, and Pa had been so proud of him. Hannah remembered Pa's beaming smile, the affectionate way he rumpled Seth's hair, the catch in his voice when he praised him. She remembered because she had yearned for such praise, but she had been sick in bed, hardly better than Pa.

Now Joel was bearing up in the same manner, running the farm, helping Mama. Steady, strong Joel. Hannah was pretty sure if Pa could see him, Joel would receive the same words of confidence and appreciation. But would she?

"Hannah!" Mr. Covington shouted from across the room. "I told you three times that I'm finished for the day. You're a million miles away, girl."

She rose and stretched her back. "Guess I am." She leaned the rake in the corner and hung the hat on it.

"Were you off on some wild journey where you were free of household chores?" he asked mockingly, plucking coins off his palm and handing them to her.

She shook her head. "Not this time. More like where the guns roar like thunder and camp chores abound."

"Hmm." He paused, frowning. "Heard from your father yet?"

She shook her head and he brushed his fingertips over his beard. "Well," he harrumphed, dismissing the subject, "nothing we can do. We're finished. But before you leave, I have something I want you to do for me. Come here."

She followed him behind the canvas he had worked on for the past hour. To her surprise, it remained completely blank.

"I want you to give this to your father, from one soldier to another." He held out a small oval disc with a minia-

109

ture portrait painted on it. It was a picture of her looking lost in thought.

She stared in complete astonishment. "This is what you were painting today?"

"Well, I certainly wasn't mopping the floor. Are you going to take it or not?"

She picked it up carefully, imagining her father's response when he received it. "Why?"

"Never mind why. I told you, it's from one soldier to another."

"But you're not—" She stopped. She'd been wrong about him once already today. She'd best bite her tongue for a change.

"I'm not a soldier?" he asked. "Look here." He fumbled around in a stack of canvases and finally pulled one out bearing a portrait of a middle-aged man in a shell jacket with a forage cap under one arm. "That's me in 1846, during the Mexican War. I kept it all these years. I still have the uniform, too, but only the hat still fits."

He propped it up against a flowery sofa and glowered down into the younger man's eyes.

Hannah felt like she'd just opened a book after staring a long while at its cover. She never imagined Mr. Covington as anything other than the cantankerous old artist he had become. But he had lived a whole life before she was even born.

"So you do understand about war," she admitted, thinking back to a past conversation.

"I understand plenty," he groused. "I've seen enough killing for three lifetimes, but the young ones, they always need to learn for themselves.

"I was asked to take a commission—at my age!—because the North needs officers so badly. But I won't do it. This war is foolish and frivolous and I want no part of it. Besides," he added, "I've got kin in the South and no wish

110

to meet them in battle."

She looked down at the miniature. "My pa will appreciate this."

"Of course he will. That's why I did it. Now go home. I need a smoke, and I'm tired of babysitting."

Chapter Twelve

"How's your brother?" Hannah whispered across the mathematics text she shared with Wes.

The weeks of hard choring had dwindled with December's first snow, and the short winter days now filled themselves with indoor tasks like spinning wool, weaving cloth, sharpening tools, mending harnesses...and school. Hannah had only returned a few days ago, but already she anticipated the end of the term.

Wes ducked so the blond head of Mary Burns blocked Miss West's line of vision. "Marcus is okay. He's been working some at Mr. Van Volkenburg's mercantile."

"Is he any happier?"

Wes shrugged. "He never jokes around anymore. And he spends a lot of time staring into the bottom of a tankard."

She doodled on her tablet. She'd only finished four problems in the last twenty minutes. "He needs to stay busy. I bet he could relearn how to do a lot of things one-handed."

"Hannah," Miss West called from the front of the room. "Slide across the aisle and sit with Sue Ellen, please."

"Sorry, Miss West." She collected her pencil and tablet.

The older girl made room with a welcoming smile. Hannah's greeting more closely resembled a grimace.

"Since you will have to wait for Wesley to finish his arithmetic before you can use the text, you may start on today's spelling assignment."

"Yes, Miss West." Spelling was her worst subject.

The school day crawled past more slowly than a turtle with a broken leg. Sue Ellen waded through her schoolwork with singular purpose, and Hannah had no doubt that in another year or two the girl would qualify to teach a school of her own. But Hannah had no such ambitions. She spent the greater part of the morning leaning on her elbow watching wisps of white clouds shred on the spindly fingers of the oak tree.

At twelve o'clock exactly Miss West rose. "You are dismissed for lunch."

Children scrambled to grab wraps and be the first one out of the schoolhouse, and Hannah jockeyed in their midst. But over the hubbub, the teacher called out, "Hannah, may I see you for a moment?"

Hannah's posture melted like sugar icing left too long by a stove. She slumped to the front of the room to await her chastisement.

"I'm not sending you to the gallows," Miss West quipped. "Mr. Briggs simply asked me to tell you there is a letter waiting for you at the post office."

Hannah sprang for the coatroom and whisked on her heavy shawl. "Thank you, Miss West!" she shouted over her shoulder.

It took only moments to scuttle through the snow to the little toll booth where Mr. Briggs sat on his stool looking between his knees at a mail-order seed catalog. Hannah was certain he'd watched her slipping all the way up the Plank Road, but he feigned surprise at her appearance. "Why, hello, Hannah! School let out already?"

113

"It's lunchtime, Mr. Briggs."

He pulled at the gold watch fob and consulted his timepiece. "Well so it is," he announced grandly. "The noon stage is due any minute."

He gazed toward Allegan and Hannah shifted impatiently. "Miss West said you have a letter for me."

"Certainly, I do. It's right here." He drew a crisp, white envelope from a stack on his desk. "Looks important too."

While Mr. Briggs looked on curiously, Hannah read the return address with disappointment. "Mercurial Landholdings, Albany, New York." It wasn't from Pa.

"Can't figure what some fancy pants eastern firm wants with your pa."

Hannah shrugged. "I don't know and I don't care. Mama and Joel can open it."

"That's probably wise," he agreed, looking just a bit crestfallen. "Funny thing, though. I've seen two more letters just the same as that addressed to other folks."

His eyebrows bunched together as he chewed on the mystery, and Hannah knew it would plague him till he discovered the answer.

Coming out of the post office, Hannah saw Marcus sitting on the porch of the hotel clad in heavy flannel. He slouched listlessly, long legs pushing his chair back against the wall, a cigarette in his hand. An empty sleeve dangled at his side. He hadn't even bothered to pin it.

"Hi, Marcus!" she called, waving cheerfully.

He turned toward her blankly, took a long drag of smoke, and looked away.

Back in the schoolyard, Hannah slipped the envelope among her books and went in search of her lunch bucket. Justin had left her only an apple and half a ham sandwich. She grabbed up both and went in search of Wes.

She found him crouched behind the woodpile, lobbing

snowballs at Danny Woodrow and Trevor Coops and making explosion sounds each time they hit the ground. The younger boys danced at the edge of his range, but a powdery dusting in Danny's dark hair testified to Wes's good aim.

Hannah bit into her sandwich. "What are you doing?"

"General Grant, your reinforcements arrived just in time," he called. "I have Jackson on my left and Longstreet on my right. My artillery is keeping them at bay, but I'm hard pressed without you. Take the left flank."

She took another bite of her sandwich and watched Trevor laugh as his snow bomb burst in front of Wes, spattering him with icy fragments. She wondered briefly if Marcus had lost his arm to shrapnel.

"Well, aren't you going to help?" Wes would get no medals for patience.

She shrugged. "When I'm done with my lunch."

He threw her an odd look. She was usually much quicker to join these adventures. "Eat fast, Mr. Grant."

But Hannah couldn't summon any enthusiasm for the game. Instead, she strolled to the front steps, bit thoughtfully into the apple, and sat down beside Sue Ellen to wait for Miss West's bell.

***

Maddy stirred a kettle of soup over the cook stove. Hannah could now see a gentle bulge rounding out the front of her dress. It was fashionable to hide a pregnancy as long as possible, and when it became obvious, to hide oneself away until the baby was born, but she thought the practice was downright silly. Of course everyone knew anyway. And it was entirely impractical when there was so much work to do.

"It's about time you got home," Maddy groused.

115

"Punch down this bread dough so I can run after some potatoes."

Hannah looked up at her sister in surprise. It was the first order Maddy had given since Tommy died. She grinned. Then she refused to comply. "The dough will keep," she answered saucily and helped herself to a handful of cookies.

Maddy clanged the spoon against the kettle harder than necessary, but Hannah had chores of her own to do. For starters, there was a whole jug of cream in the root cellar that Mama wanted churned tonight. But as she left the cellar with the jug, she softened and filled her skirt with potatoes.

Hannah settled at the kitchen table with her school books and plunged the churn's handle up and down, up and down as she read. She switched hands a score of times and finished her homework before the cream finally congealed. Setting her books aside, she poured the buttermilk into a pitcher on the table. Then, using a wooden paddle, she worked the butter until all the liquid squeezed out. By the time it was rinsed and scooped into molds, darkness had fallen and Maddy was calling the family in for dinner.

Mama came in first. Her face looked pale and lined, and she shivered violently. The old malady. But this time there was something more, a rasping sound that rattled out of her chest with every breath.

Hannah jumped up. "Mama, you look terrible! Want me to fetch Doc Graves?"

Mama waved her off and stumbled toward her bedroom. "No, no. It's just a touch of the ague. I'll be fine, but I don't feel much like dinner. Tell Joel I left the milk in the barn. I was afraid I'd splash it all over the yard if I tried to lift it."

"All right, Mama." Hannah watched her go, and as the others filed wordlessly to the table, she set water on for tea and spread a slice of warm bread thickly with butter, knowing all the time that Mama probably wouldn't touch it. Only the sound of chewing and the clink of silverware on plates was audible, but the room throbbed with strain. It was mighty late in the year for summer sickness.

Hannah brought the tray in to her mother. When she returned she confessed, "I'm worried about her, Joel."

Justin blew it off. "Mama gets the fever and ague all the time."

"Not like this."

Joel nodded. "I'll get some quinine from Doc after dinner."

"Can we afford it?" Maddy asked.

Joel stared hard at her. "We have to afford it."

"That reminds me," Hannah said, rummaging among her school books. "I picked up a letter today from some business in New York. It's addressed to Pa."

Joel took the envelope and studied it some before ripping open the flap. He withdrew a single, crisply folded page, and as he read his face grew dark. Then he wadded it into a tight ball and threw it on the table.

"What is it?" Justin had to know.

"Lawson duped us."

Three sets of eyes stared blankly at him.

"What do you mean?" Maddy ventured.

"It's a letter from Lawson, a demand for payment. It says if we don't cough up the money by the end of the year, he gets the deed to our farm."

"But I thought he told Mama we could work out arrangements if we couldn't raise the money by the end of the year," Hannah pleaded. "I thought he wanted to help us."

"I thought so, too." Joel ground his teeth. "Blast! How could we have been so stupid?"

But Hannah wasn't ready to suspect the friendly shopkeeper. "Maybe this is just a misunderstanding. Maybe if we

117

pay him a visit we can get to the bottom of it."

"That's exactly what I intend to do," Joel stated.

***

The children chose not to tell Mama about the letter. Leaving Maddy behind to care for her, Joel left for town, hitching up the cart for Hannah and Justin who insisted on coming along.

They stopped at Doc Graves' house first. The old man cheerfully prepared some medicine.

"Keep her warm as always, and try to get liquids down her. When it changes to fever, sponge her with lukewarm water. Let me know if she isn't feeling better very soon."

They moved on quickly to Mr. Lawson's.

The store was dark. Joel pounded on the front door. "Lawson, you in there?" His breath clouded in icy puffs that faded with his words.

As Hannah stared up at the cold, unlit windows in the apartment, a chill darkness seeped under her wraps and froze up solid in her chest. She couldn't believe Mr. Lawson would betray them. Part of her wanted to scream in his face and pound on his barrel chest with her fists. Another part dreaded the confrontation. And a third still hoped it was all just a simple misunderstanding. But as they waited in silence, a growing realization began to spread over her.

Mr. Lawson was gone.

Rounder nuzzled Hannah's cheek and snorted his concern through wide nostrils. Hannah reached out to hug his neck, glad to lean against the horse's strong, warm shoulder.

Joel pounded again. "Lawson!" he shouted. "Lawson, open up!"

Justin and Hannah added their own voices till Mrs. Clark charged out her front door. "What's the meaning of all this racket? You sound like a pack of alley cats yowling in the street."

Hannah rushed up to her. "Mrs. Clark, do you know where we can find Mr. Lawson?"

"Lawson? Haven't seen him since yesterday. Packed a wagon and headed toward Hilliards."

"Do you know when he'll be back?"

"Do I look like his secretary?"

"Please, Mrs. Clark, you must know something."

The old woman peered through oversized spectacles. "If I told you, would you hold off howling outside my door?"

"Of course. We'll go straight home like proper children."

"Well then," she told them, "don't look for Lawson to come back."

Hannah's heart dropped. She had known it.

But Joel needed further proof. "What makes you say that? Maybe he's just off on a visit."

Mrs. Clark shook her head. "No visit. He's cleared out. Loaded that wagon till there was nothing left in his store. And then he packed up that big orange cat. Plunked it in a basket and wedged it in the wagon and lit out." She shook her head again. "He's not coming back. I never did like that man."

The children stared at each other for a long moment. Finally Joel said, "Thank you, Mrs. Clark."

She harrumphed. "Get along home now, all of you. It's freezing out here."

They straggled into the cart in defeat. Rounder's hooves clopped loudly in the darkness.

"Now what?" Hannah moped.

"I'm going to pay a visit to Mr. Thomas and see if there's any way out of this mess." His voice sounded as tight as a piano wire, and Hannah knew he blamed himself.

Mr. Thomas was commonly regarded as the local authority on matters of law because he once worked as a legal assistant in Connecticut before moving west to try farming. His children were all grown up and moved away, except one daughter who had married the shoemaker and lived in town. A single light shone in the kitchen window. Joel knocked apologetically.

"Sorry for intruding on you so late, Mrs. Thomas," he said when the woman opened the door, "but we really need to speak to your husband. Is he in?"

The lady swung the door wide. "Yes, come in. My, three of you? I hope everything's all right. Is your mother well?"

"She's down with the fever," Joel answered, "but that's not why we're here. I was wondering if I could show something to your husband."

"Of course. I'll call him."

The children hovered near the cook stove, exposing pink skin to the heat still radiating from it. As they warmed, Hannah's fingers grew fuzzy and prickly, as if massaged by a score of tiny-clawed mice.

Mr. Thomas strode into the room with trousers pulled hastily over long underwear. He was short and wiry and looked like every other farmer in Allegan County. "Hello, Joel, Hannah, Justin," he called, securing the straps of his suspenders over his shoulders.

Joel nodded a greeting for all of them.

"What can I help you children with?"

Joel pulled the wrinkled letter from his pocket. "A few weeks ago we signed loan papers with Mr. Lawson."

"Of course, of course. Good man, Lawson." Mr. Thomas pulled up a chair.

"We thought so too." Joel handed the letter to Mr. Thomas and sat across from him. "Until we received this in the mail today."

The farmer threaded his eyeglasses over his ears and

hummed to himself as he read. Then he peered at them over the top of the lenses. "Do you have a copy of the loan?"

Joel produced it.

Mr. Thomas scanned the pages briefly, and his face turned thoughtful. "It's all in order, unfortunately. It seems our Mr. Lawson is something other than what he appeared."

Hannah was indignant. "But he said we could have more time to pay the loan."

"I'm afraid a verbal agreement isn't obligatory. But this contract," he shook the pages, "is signed by both parties and binding in any court of law. I'm sorry."

A muscle clenched in Joel's jaw. "But what does any of this have to do with Mercurial Landholdings?"

"I suspect Mercurial is a speculating company that Lawson owns or works for. They buy up land as cheaply as possible and sell it at a profit. You'll recall Lawson was pretty keen on the railroad going through, driving up land values. I'd be willing to bet he set up more of these loans to other folks just like yourselves—trusting folks struggling to make ends meet—with the intention of gaining their land."

Joel's eyes screwed up and his lips pinched together. "You mean Mr. Lawson's part of a land racket?"

"Well, I'd say he's a scoundrel, but this is all legal I'm afraid. If these loans default, Lawson picks up a lot of land cheap. If they don't, he makes a little interest and he's not out anything. It's too bad," Mr. Thomas added. "I liked him, but he duped us all."

"But Mr. Lawson set up shop, got involved in the community, made friends. Why would he spend a year with us only to sell us out?" Joel asked.

"Maybe he never came with such intentions. It's possible he just spotted the opportunity and acted on it." Thomas shrugged. "But most likely he's been scoping out the area, quietly buying up all the land he could get his hands on, and

121

procuring the rest by whatever means worked."

Justin piped up. "Mr. Lawson's gone. We just stopped at his place, but the store is empty. Mrs. Clark said she saw him leave town yesterday."

"I'll bet he did. He'd face a lynching if he stayed."

"I just can't believe it of him," Joel said glumly.

"Well, I can," Hannah stormed. White-hot fire coursed through her veins. "If I ever see him again, why I'll—"

Justin grinned. "You'll what, slug him in the stomach? You might just about reach it."

"I don't know what," she glowered. "But I'll tell you one thing. If I have to walk to New York, Mr. Lawson will not be getting our farm!"

Chapter Thirteen

Doctor Graves closed the door softly and lowered himself into a kitchen chair. "It's a classic case of whooping cough, I'm afraid."

The anxiety that had boiled Hannah's stomach into pudding finally cooled. Quinine had cut short Mama's chills and fever days ago, but her breathing had declined into great consuming coughs that racked her body till Hannah feared consumption. Whooping cough was a serious condition, one that would take weeks to recover from, but it carried no death sentence. Hannah saw her relief mirrored around the table in the faces of her siblings.

"Is it catching?" Maddy asked.

"It's extremely contagious, and deadly in young children, so you will have to make arrangements for Justin to move in with friends immediately."

"I'm not leaving," Justin stated firmly, but no one paid him any mind.

"I'm sure he could stay with Mrs. Patton," Hannah suggested.

"Very good."

"I'm not leaving!"

"You are leaving," Joel said firmly. Then he ruffled the little boy's hair. "But don't think I'm letting you out of work. The girls and I can't run this farm by ourselves."

Justin brightened.

The doctor cleared his throat. "I'm afraid you'll have to do it without Maddy. She's in no condition to take such a risk." There was a long pause as the doctor looked from Hannah to Joel. In the silence, they could hear Mama's rasping coughs as she fought for breath in the next room.

Maddy looked away out the window, her face grown stiff and emotionless. "I suppose I could move in with my in-laws."

Hannah's heart sank. Could three children run the farm alone? Could they nurse Mama, care for the stock, cook, clean, do the mending, the washing, the endless chores—alone?

"Perhaps we could find you some help in town," the old man suggested.

But Joel shored up his shoulders. "We'll manage. It's a slow time of year. Anything that doesn't have to get done till spring can wait till spring."

Justin added proudly, "Yeah, me and Joel can take care of things."

Hannah looked from one brother to the other, Joel with his broad shoulders and unruffled demeanor, Justin with a stubborn set to his jaw and a light in his eyes, and she lifted her own chin. They would all make Pa proud together. "We'll be all right, Doctor Graves."

The doctor smiled slowly and looked around at each face. "I believe you will."

He laid a tin of powders and a colored glass vial on the table and gave them meticulous instructions. "If she gets worse, or if you need any help, don't hesitate to call for me."

The old man reached for his bag, paused, and turned to

them with a sigh. "You kids have enough trouble..." His eyes were wells of pity. "There's been another battle. In Fredericksburg, Virginia. A terrible one. I'm afraid our army didn't fare well." He groped for his bag. "I hate to have to tell you, but I thought you'd want to know."

***

Mama's condition worsened until she was seized with bouts of gagging, even vomiting, from the violence of her coughing fits. The whites of her eyes turned red as blood vessels ruptured, and the precious liquids that kept life in her flowed into the bedpan faster than Hannah could replace them with broth and milk and hot tea.

Every few hours Hannah carefully administered pecacuanha powder and tincture of belladonna and even a sedative made from camphor and opium, but nothing seemed to help. And as Mama grew worse, Hannah grew increasingly exhausted.

The boys tended the stock, carried water, filled the wood box, and brought in all the food items Hannah requested. Joel even boiled and hung the ever-growing pile of laundry. Hannah didn't have to step outside for anything, but she also didn't see the sun for two weeks. She rose with the darkness of morning, toiled through the short hours of daylight, stopping only to eat two simple meals with Joel, and dropped into bed long after nightfall. She spoke to no one except Joel, Mama, and the doctor.

Occasionally she spotted Justin outside the window. And once Mrs. Stockdale delivered a mincemeat pie and some blueberry preserves and a letter from Maddy, but she didn't stay for tea. Hannah could hardly blame her, though she longed for just twenty minutes of conversation.

Another time Mrs. Carver brought a stew and paid her a short visit while Mr. Carver helped Joel repair a broken door on the barn, but they didn't stay long either. Even good friends like the Carvers didn't want to linger at a sick house.

But at least they had come. There'd been no sign of Wes.

One morning, in the third week of Mama's illness, Hannah sliced up a loaf of bread with the last of Mrs. Stockdale's preserves and poured a cup of strong, hot coffee. She sank wearily into a chair. The thought of another long, lonely day made her want to crawl back into bed and pull a pillow over her head, but she faced Joel bravely.

"The loan comes due in two weeks," she reminded him.

He nodded. "I sold the yearling sheep last week, and Mrs. Patton said she'd keep the milk cow till we can afford to buy her back."

"There goes our butter money."

"We'll make it," he assured her. He looked absolutely certain.

"How much do we still owe?"

"About seventy-five dollars."

Her heart plunged. How could he look so calm? How could he be so sure? "I wish we hadn't paid Mr. Lawson's store credit off."

Joel laughed. "It wouldn't have been enough. We'd still have to sell off more stock."

"Not the horses, Joel! We can't make a living if we sell the plow horses."

"Not the plow horses," he agreed as he left the table. "Don't worry. We'll make it."

But darkness, stress, and exhaustion all fought against Joel's confident words. She did worry. After all their struggle, after Pa and Seth volunteered to serve in the war, after they had worked and sweated and strained and tried, they were going to lose their farm. It just wasn't fair.

Blackness gripped Hannah. She threw a chair over backwards and cursed the war. Forgetting her mother's ears in the next room, she swore at Mr. Lincoln, at the Confederacy, and at the colored slaves at the heart of the conflict. She thrashed them roundly, up one wall and down another until she slumped into the chair, as drained as an empty kettle.

Defeat after defeat after defeat. The names of faraway battlefields, once so glamorous and exciting, tolled through her memory like the clanging of a church bell. Seven Pines, Shiloh, Bull Run, Antietam, and now Fredericksburg. They were claiming men like Pa who had worked so hard to build the country, destroying their families, draining the blood of American pioneers. And at the end of it all—if Pa came home at all—he wouldn't even have a bit of land to call his own.

She was tottering on the edge of that black place in her mind where fear, worry, and the unknown all mixed together in a deadly poison when a knock at the door startled her back to reality. Rubbing her hands over her face, she took a deep breath and threw the door wide.

"Hello, Hannah." Sue Ellen stood on the snowy stoop holding a loaf of bread and a bucket of soup. The towel thrown over its top couldn't contain the steamy aroma.

Hannah managed a smile and reached for the food. "Thank you, Sue Ellen. I appreciate your kindness." She began tugging the door closed, but the girl stopped it with an open palm.

"Aren't you going to invite me in?"

Hannah blinked. "What?"

"I want to come in."

"But—are you sure? It's catching in here."

Sue Ellen laughed and stepped in uninvited. "I'll risk it. I've no younger siblings to carry it home to. You look terrible," she added as she donned Mama's apron and promptly began clearing breakfast dishes.

Hannah stood in the doorway, still holding the steaming bucket, and watched stupidly as Sue Ellen filled a basin with hot water. "Why are you doing this?"

Sue Ellen shrugged. "Doc said you need help. And I hardly ever catch anything, so Mama finally let me come. Oh," the girl said, turning to her, "I spoke with Mr. Covington in town and he wanted me to tell you he's coming today at two o'clock sharp. He says he has to get his paintings shipped to New York by the end of the year, but he can't finish the last one without you."

"Doesn't he know he could get sick?"

Sue Ellen gave a breezy wave. "He said he's too ornery to catch it."

"He is," Hannah chuckled. It sounded rusty.

She watched as Sue Ellen scrubbed up the few dishes then started in on the floor. The girl really wasn't going away. Hannah sank to a chair with gratitude.

"That is a very practical fashion you are wearing," Sue Ellen commented with a dimpled smile.

Hannah looked down. She had on Seth's trousers and an old shirtwaist of Maddy's. It did look pretty silly.

"Practical," Sue Ellen continued, "but not very feminine. Perhaps we could embroider some flowers on your britches to tell them apart from your brother's."

Hannah scowled, embarrassed, before she realized Sue Ellen was making a joke. She chuckled again then laughed out loud.

Soon the kitchen floor glistened like it hadn't in weeks. Sue Ellen stood up and surveyed it with a critical eye. "Good. Now how about these windows?" But first she placed the bucket of soup on the stove where it would keep warm.

Why hadn't Hannah noticed before how kind the girl was?

She knew why, of course. She'd never needed Sue Ellen's friendship. She always had Mary Ann, and then Wes. Now the girl's unexpected presence blazed like a light in a dark, musty closet. And like a cockroach suddenly exposed, Hannah's discouragement scurried back into the far corners of her mind. Together the girls accomplished four times the work Hannah had hoped to do alone.

At noon, Joel joined them for bowls of the best-tasting chicken vegetable soup Hannah could remember eating. Or perhaps it had just been so long since her last good meal. Or maybe it was the cheerful company.

Sue Ellen popped up from her chair. "Hannah, you still look tired. I'll wash up these dishes then start in on that basket of mending. You go take a short rest before Mr. Covington gets here. We don't want all of New York City seeing you look like a goblin."

Hannah was only too willing to comply. As she left the table, she noticed that Joel, for once, seemed in no hurry to return to his chores. And she was trying to recall why she never liked Sue Ellen.

***

A rough pounding woke Hannah with a start. She flew down the stairs to open the door before the noise disturbed her mother, but Sue Ellen had already admitted Mr. Covington. He stood filling the entryway with his easel, canvas, and paints.

"Good afternoon, Mr. Covington," she greeted. He grunted, raking her with a questioning eye. With a flush of embarrassment, she recalled her trousers.

"I can go change," she mumbled.

"Now hold on. That might be just the thing..." He rubbed at his chin with one hand, one eye screwed up tight. "Yes, it's simply brilliant! You're the picture of a country

129

girl making do in time of war. The folks back home will love it."

"They won't be scandalized?" she asked skeptically.

"No doubt, no doubt. But they'll get over it. And then they'll find it quaint. Perfectly quaint."

He held up a partially finished painting of a horse in a box stall with sparkling eye and arched neck and snow on the barn window. Hannah could almost feel the animal's frosty breath. "Mr. Covington..." she breathed.

He held up a warning finger. "Remember our agreement." She bit back a smile. "Now, if you'll throw on a shawl and accompany me to the barn, I'll proceed to paint you leaning against the half door."

The barn smelled of hay, manure, and old timbers—a sweet, wholesome fragrance. Mr. Covington promptly positioned her with an arm draped across the top of Rounder's stall door. As she gazed in at him, Rounder sauntered over to investigate. Hannah rubbed the white spot between his eyes.

"This is my pa's horse," she said. Then she gave a caustic smile. "At least it was. I don't even know if Pa's dead or alive. We've heard nothing for weeks." When she allowed herself to speak about it, her buried fears welled up suddenly, like venom leaking from an old wound.

Mr. Covington glanced up as he painted. "I heard the seventeenth wasn't a part of the last battle."

"Rumors," she spat out, surprised at her own bitterness. "Nobody knows anything for sure after both sides are done slaughtering each other. It takes weeks to sort out the details, and even then nothing's certain. He could be dead on the battlefield, unidentified, and we might never know it."

Rounder nudged her gently, questioningly, with his muzzle. She cupped a hand over the soft warmth. "Of course, it might be better if he died without knowing how

I've let him down."

"What sort of rubbish are you talking about, girl?"

The sting of her anger vanished, replaced by empty hopelessness. "I've failed him, Mr. Covington. Just before he left, he told me to take care of things while he was gone."

She could still see her father standing there outside the barn door, wearing his good suit and holding some personal items wrapped up in an old pillowcase. He had hugged her and kissed the top of her head. "*Remember, Peanut, be brave. I love you, and I'm counting on you. When I come home, I expect to see everything just as I left it.*"

It was the last thing he had said to her.

She turned to the artist. "I let him down. I've lost the farm."

Mr. Covington set down his brush and regarded her shrewdly. "So, you failed to control that hailstorm, did you?" His words were sharp. "And you could have influenced market prices? And why didn't you do a better job dictating the actions of that scoundrel, Lawson?"

She looked at him wonderingly.

"Bah, the story's all over town."

He picked up his brush and focused again on the tiny strokes. "You've been climbing broken ladders ever since I've known you. Running from reality, chasing shadowy dreams, trying your darnedest to be some kind of hero. You can't do the impossible, child."

Hannah turned back to face Rounder. He had moved to the trough and was pulling up wisps of hay and munching them happily.

Mr. Covington's words poured out harsh and unpleasant, but as always, she found they were true. And though they were meant to relieve her, to lessen the pressure she put on herself, they made her feel worse. She couldn't hope to do the impossible. She couldn't save the farm. Her father, when he returned—if he returned—would have to start all over again somewhere else. She felt as broken as Mr. Covington's ladder.

She watched Rounder arch his neck at some noise in the farmyard. His ears pricked forward, his eyes focused intently on something outside the door. He was breathtakingly beautiful, and the sharp look in his eye proclaimed his intelligence. He was an extremely valuable animal.

Her eyes grew round. Of course! If everything else failed, they could sell Rounder. Why had she never thought of it before?

But even as the thought entered her head, her stomach squeezed in rebellion. Rounder was Pa's horse. He loved Rounder. She loved Rounder. It would be a betrayal.

But if it would save the farm...

When Mr. Covington finished his painting, he packed up his equipment and tucked his brushes in his pocket. Pulling his hand out, he gave her a thick envelope. "Briggs asked me to deliver this."

Hannah recognized her father's handwriting. Not waiting to see the artist on his way, she raced to the house and tore open the packet.

It contained one thin note from Seth and an entire stack of letters from her father, tied neatly with a bit of string. Pa's were arranged in order, starting way back in September, and Hannah knew they would be full of pictures, stories, and snippets of camp life. She set them aside to savor with her family later. Seth's, however, she unfolded immediately. He wrote much less, but he always included the news she was most anxious to hear, and he did not fail her this time.

November 20, 1862
Dear Mama and everyone,

I'm sorry I haven't written more, but my hand has been pretty sore. I'll try to catch you up now.

132

Soon after Antietam, our regiment left Maryland, crossing the Potomac River to Waterford, Virginia where we encamped for some time. There we learned that McClellan had been relieved of command. My joy was great till I learned who would be our new commander: Burnside, the same idiot who tried his darnedest to destroy our corps at the Antietam Creek bridge.

Burnside moved us on to Falmouth with plans to cross the Rappahannock and surprise the enemy. But our pontoon bridges were delayed, and instead of fording the river as we should have done, the old fool waited for weeks to cross till the enemy was well dug in on the heights across the river.

(The delay had one advantage. We received your package in Falmouth, and our stockings and mufflers have kept us in good stead. It does not get as cold here as it does at home, but the wind blows through a man, particularly during picket duty.)

Pa is not well. He has fought as hard as any other man, uncomplaining, hanging on despite poor health. But the marching, exposure, his age, and dysentery have wiped him out. He's exhausted. He won't tell you, but he's been in and out of the hospital half a dozen times. Our sergeant is working to get him released from the service altogether.

Pa's a bad case, but everybody's sick. Camp is cold and dirty, and most everybody has some kind of intestinal ailment, so it stinks, too. Outbreaks of measles and smallpox spread like wildfire. Then there's pneumonia, tuberculosis, typhoid, whooping cough. If the Rebs knew how disease was aiding their cause, they could sit back and wait out the war. But I suppose they are faring the same.

But don't worry, Mama. I'm one of the lucky ones. Aside from a bit of the flux and a deserting finger, I'm fine. Even well. But I miss you all.

> Your son,
> Seth Wallace

Chapter Fourteen

Two weeks before Christmas, Mama's coughing fits began to ease. She still looked weak and as pale as the sheet she lay on, but her breathing regulated and her food stayed down. A well-pleased Doctor Graves declared that the other children could move back in soon after the New Year. They would celebrate Christmas together then.

Hannah's burden lightened tremendously. Sue Ellen appeared on the doorstep every few days and set herself to household tasks as though she lived there. The dogged persistence Hannah had always scorned in the girl now earned her admiration, and tasks that had overwhelmed her became as pleasant as a spring walk under the older girl's steady hand. The house sparkled, wonderful smells filled the kitchen, and three hot meals covered the table once again.

Only one worry haunted Hannah's mind—money.

Joel seemed confident they would be able pay off the loan, but he never seemed inclined to talk about it. He did a little hunting and trapping, though Hannah knew the bit he earned could never cover what was owed, and the uncertainty made her tense and irritable.

Three days before Christmas, Hannah kneaded a batch

of bread dough, punching it with an increasing violence that rattled the table until Sue Ellen stepped in with a gentle touch on her shoulder. "You haven't been outside for days," she suggested. "Why don't you take a walk? I can manage the bread."

Hannah didn't need much persuasion. Bundled in scarf and mittens and two pairs of woolen stockings, she stomped across the barnyard. The snow lay several inches deep, and an icy crust had formed on top after a day of moderate temperatures. She set off without any destination in mind.

Her footsteps took her down the road she had followed when she drove the Pattons' horses home only a few months ago. She walked along the smooth, hard-packed sleigh tracks, passing the spot where Mr. Covington had fallen over and bungled his painting, and paused at the edge of a tiny, spring-fed lake. Ice had formed around its edge, though a flock of Canadian geese swam in the middle, apparently in no hurry to fly south.

A noise in the underbrush startled her. She dodged behind a tree, aware that she was very near the spot where she and Wes had seen the bear.

But it wasn't a bear. It was Wes.

The boy was ducked low, hiding behind an enormous stump, peering in the opposite direction.

Hannah tiptoed to within a wagon's length of him and shouted, "Wesley Carver!"

He jumped as high as a jackrabbit.

Hannah giggled. "What are you doing here, Wes?"

"Quiet!" he hissed, leaping to clap a mitten over her mouth.

"Why?" she whispered through the wet yarn.

A voice carried through the forest. "I see you on my flank, Grant!"

Hannah could just make out a figure through the trees. It looked like Danny Woodrow.

135

"Aw," Wes grumbled, "you ruined my surprise attack." He called to the boy in the wood, "Don't try anything foolish, General Jackson. My reinforcements just arrived." Then he began issuing orders to Hannah.

"Quick, move around to his left flank. I'll go to his right. I've become General Grant in your absence, so you'll have to settle for Burnside. Sorry."

After Seth's letter, she had no desire to play General Burnside. And after everything else that had happened, the sport seemed like a silly, childish fantasy, unimportant and disconnected from real life.

"You're still playing games?" she asked.

Wes looked up in surprise. He studied her face. "What do you want me to do? Stay at home and mope with my brother?"

"Of course not. But I thought you might have a little consideration."

He shrugged. "It wouldn't change anything. Marcus is determined to be unhappy. I'm not going to let him ruin my fun."

He turned back to his sport, and she kicked at a clump of snow. "I've been gone from school for a month. Why haven't you come to visit?" she asked.

"Are you kidding?" he gaped, turning around. "And catch what your ma has?" He shook his head like the answer should have been obvious.

"We could have met in the barn," she countered, "or talked in the yard. Didn't you even wonder how I was?"

"Ma gives me updates. Come on, General Burnside. If we move out we can squeeze Jackson between us."

Hannah stood rooted to the spot, watching Wes until he disappeared into the trees. Then with an odd sense of loss, as though she had grown and stretched and left a part of herself behind, she turned for home.

Sue Ellen was gone by the time she arrived. Joel met

136

Hannah in the yard as if he'd been waiting for her. "Mama's awake. I think we need to talk to her."

He tried to usher her inside, but the episode with Wes had left her gloomy and miserable. She jerked her arm away harder than she intended. "I'll come in when I'm good and ready," she snapped.

She followed him in and took her wraps off with slow deliberation. Only after each one hung neatly on its peg did she enter the bedroom.

Mama smiled at her. Her cheeks looked thin and drawn, but they were pink again. "Hannah, you've been an angel. I don't know how you've managed everything at your age, but you have. You and Joel both."

"And me too!"

Justin burst into the room and flung his arms around his mother.

Hannah let a growl of pure exasperation escape. "Doctor Graves said you can't be in here yet, Justin." She grabbed his arm and tried to haul him out the door, but he fought back like a devil.

"I'm not leaving!" he yelled, pounding on her forearm.

"Stop hitting me, you little cow pie!" She cuffed him on the ear, and he clobbered her on the cheek. With a gasp of surprise, she retaliated with handfuls of his hair. He yowled, and his fingers latched onto her wrists and dug in.

"Enough!" Joel yanked each of them by an ear. Hannah had never seen his face so livid. His eyes snapped fire. "Even after three weeks apart, you two set in on each other like a pack of wolves the moment you see each other. And in Mama's room, too! You ought to be ashamed of yourselves."

He shoved them into opposite corners. "I don't understand why you must always be at each other's throats. You're family, for pity's sake."

Hannah glowered, holding her smarting cheek. "It's

137

him. He acts like he's royalty and the rest of us are just stupid, useless peasants. I'm fed up with his attitude. I'm fed up with him! He shouldn't even be in this house yet."

"Hannah," Joel warned, "Justin has a right to be here. He's been working like a man for weeks."

Justin beamed triumphantly under his brother's praise.

Hannah's eyes blazed. "I have scrubbed and cooked and nursed until my body ached. I slept on the sofa when I didn't have strength left to climb the stairs. Don't tell me he worked harder than I did."

"No one said he worked harder." Joel pressed a fist against his forehead in exasperation.

"Hannah." Mama spoke softly from the bed. "I'd like a cup of tea, if you don't mind."

Hannah's eyes narrowed to angry slits, and she whirled from the room. How she hated Justin! She'd like to wring his scrawny neck!

She slammed the kettle on the stove and rattled the china on the tea tray until Mama called out, "Hannah, please be careful. Those were my mother's dishes." The effort set her to coughing again.

Hannah flopped sulkily into a chair and laid her head on her arms. She could have easily dissolved into tears, but she wouldn't give Justin that satisfaction. She'd get back at him instead. She'd show him once and for all—she'd show everyone—that Hannah Wallace could live up to any member of the family, dead or alive. She'd leave no doubt!

Abandoning the tea, she slipped out the door.

***

Hannah approached the post office, her purpose set.

"Hello, Hannah. Got a letter to send out?" Mr. Briggs perched on his stool in front of the window as usual.

"Not this time, Mr. Briggs. I'm wondering if you know

138

of anyone who's looking to buy a good horse. He's broken to saddle and harness, and he's as sweet-tempered as a kitten."

Mr. Briggs fingered his watch fob absently as he considered. "Can't recollect anyone right off. Though I'll keep it in mind and ask around if you like."

Her stomach twisted at her task, but she ignored it.

The postmaster looked at her more carefully. "Why do you ask? Your daddy looking to sell off the farm?"

"Oh, no," she replied airily, "I just know someone who's looking to sell an animal. Thought I'd help her ask around."

"Oh? Who would that be?"

She wrinkled her nose. "I should probably let her tell you. I'm sure she'll be by in a few days herself."

"All right." He seemed pacified. "I'll keep thinking."

Next, Hannah crossed over to the hotel where a stage rested. The horses relaxed in their traces, their muzzles chuffing out steam like a row of miniature smokestacks, their hooves gouging at the snowy planks.

"Excuse me, sir," Hannah hailed the driver, patting one of the horses on its glossy neck and trying not to picture Rounder in its place. "Where does the stage purchase such fine horses?"

The man beamed at her. "That one's a beauty, ain't he now? I believe he came from a breeder down Jackson way. We get most of our animals from a few large farms. In fact, we just got a new shipment in last week. We're going to phase out some of the older animals. You interested?"

"No sir," she answered. "Just curious."

She gave the horse a last slap. Glancing around out of habit, she could see no sign of Wes or Marcus, but their absence didn't really disappoint her. Wandering across town, she entered Mr. Stockdale's smithy. He shoed every horse within eight miles and might know something.

The shop felt hot and stuffy, a welcome contrast to the frigid winter air.

"Good afternoon, Mr. Stockdale."

The smith gave her a cursory glance. "Be with you in a moment, Hannah."

He pounded a thin piece of red-hot metal with a hammer. Then he plunged the unfinished tool into a bucket of water. Steam hissed up and mingled with the smoke blackening the ceiling.

Mr. Stockdale wiped his hands on his leather apron and leaned a hip against the counter. "What can I do for you? Joel need something mended?"

"No, sir, nothing like that. I'm just wondering if you know anyone who wants to buy a good horse."

He looked at her shrewdly. "Your Pa selling that Morgan?"

Hannah looked up, startled. "Um...ah...no! Of course not! I mean, I know someone who wants to sell another horse. An excellent saddle horse. But not Rounder." She stopped, flustered.

"Well," he said with a keen eye, "not too many folks in town can afford a horse like you're describing for the money your friend probably needs. Allegan would be a better place to do business. A steady war mount sells for a fine price nowadays. If I had a dandy to sell, I'd ask Mrs. Patton who her husband's contact is in that city."

Hannah gulped. The war would be even worse than the stage!

"Thank you, Mr. Stockdale. I'll do that."

She walked home with a heavy heart.

Passing the Patton farm, Hannah found herself drawn to the paddock containing the graceful quarter horses. They scuffed through the layer of snow, scrounging for grass underneath.

Mrs. Patton emerged from the barn carrying a broad-bladed shovel. "Hello, Hannah!" she called. "Can I help you?"

"Oh, no ma'am," she replied, hopping down from the rail fence. "I'm on my way home from town, and I just stopped to admire your horses. They're so beautiful."

Mrs. Patton leaned the shovel up against the fence. "They're Josiah's pride and joy."

Hannah regarded the woman evenly. It was now or never. "He sold the others to a man in Allegan, right?"

The woman looked mildly surprised. "As a matter of fact, he did. There's a man there by the name of Edward Rochester who deals for the cavalry. He's fairly well-known."

"It must have been hard to sell them."

"Well, yes, it was. I had to tell myself it was just business."

That's what Hannah would tell herself, too, because she could not lose Pa's home. And selling Rounder was the only way to keep it. Funny how the farm she could not wait to leave such a short time ago had become the most important thing in the whole world.

She bid Mrs. Patton farewell with a plan fully formed. She was not going to sit around and wait for Mr. Lawson's company to strike. No, she was going take matters into her own hands. At last, her time had come.

She was leaving for Allegan on Rounder—tonight!

Chapter Fifteen

Shadows grew long and melted into one another before Hannah turned the white horse west at the crossroads in Martin. The new road was icy dirt, and after nine miles riding south over warping planks, Hannah wasn't disappointed to leave the highway behind. Though she had only been to Allegan one time, so many years ago, she knew this road would take her straight to the city, still ten miles away.

After leaving Mrs. Patton's farm, Hannah had sneaked up to her room. She changed into her trousers and grabbed Joel's heavy barn coat and one of his old hats. The clothing would be warmer than her own. But she stuffed a dress and a heavy shawl into a pillowcase as well, along with fresh bread from the kitchen and a tin cup.

Acting on impulse, she had set out much too late to reach Allegan by nightfall, but it would be an easy task to find a warm barn to sleep in for the night. In Allegan, she would purchase a ticket on the stage for her return—she'd always wanted to ride the stage—and be home by tomorrow evening.

Now as daylight dissolved around her, Hannah's stomach growled ravenously. Fingers that grasped the knotted reins grew numb, but she decided to plod on a few more miles. She passed a handful of houses in the village, then lights became widely scattered across the open fields.

Hannah wasn't afraid; she had camped out at night a dozen times with Seth and Joel on their imaginary journeys. But she was terribly excited. At last, she was off on a real adventure! After so much dreaming, hoping, and anticipating, she had really done it. A secret pleasure fizzed like soda water in her stomach.

The road took a curve and zigzagged for nearly a mile. Sometimes Hannah could see a skin of ice reflecting the moonlight on her left and sometimes on her right. Last summer's cattails stood in silhouette against the glow and rattled when the wind touched them. She was grateful for the frozen footing beneath Rounder's hooves. In the spring, the low areas surely grew swampy.

Without warning, the road suddenly ended. A crossroad ran north to south, but Hannah knew she must continue west for many miles. She sat shivering on the horse for a full two minutes wondering what to do.

Certainly the road just took a jog, but in what direction, and for how long? In the darkness she could see nothing. Perhaps she should retire for the night and find her way in the morning.

As she lingered, the faint sound of galloping approached from behind. It grew closer, and the pattern of two distinct hoofbeats separated themselves. Two horses.

Hannah smiled. The timing seemed providential. Surely the riders would know which direction she must take.

The horses approached quickly, recklessly. Hannah waved her arms and shouted, hoping they would see her in the dark. Then they were sliding on their haunches, fighting to stop on the slippery road. Rounder danced to one side, and the two new horses stood blowing heavily, their sides heaving in and out.

"Well, wha' 'ave we 'ere?" The voice that came from the first rider was deep and slurred, and Hannah had the impression of immense strength. "Looks like a fella lost his way, Al."

The stink of old liquor hit her, and Hannah suddenly wished she had dodged into the trees before the men approached. But it was too late now. Maybe they wouldn't be traveling her direction.

She made her voice as low as possible. "Please, I wonder if you could tell me which road leads to Allegan?" She was glad now for the deception of Joel's old clothing.

The big man chuckled. It sounded like the growl of a bull mastiff. "Sure we could, couldn't we, Al?"

"Aye, sure we could." The second voice sounded sleepy. Not as threatening. They were probably just locals on their way home from a few rounds at the inn.

"Would you please?" she prompted.

The big man circled to her other side, sandwiching Rounder in the middle. "Nice 'orse you got there. Clean lines. He'd fetch a right nice sum, wouldn't he, Al?"

"Aye, right nice."

A prickle of apprehension rolled down Hannah's spine like an icy drop of water. She prodded Rounder forward. The sleepy fellow stayed hunched over his horse, but the big one followed her stride for stride.

"Please, I need to get to Allegan."

Mastiff laughed. "Allegan's a long way from 'ere." He glanced over his shoulder. "Fact is, everything's a long way from 'ere. Ain't nothing around at all, is there, Al?"

"Aye, nothing at all."

Hannah's breath froze. It was true. She hadn't seen a single light since the road passed through the swampy lakes. She was absolutely alone with two drunken men.

Alone, except for Rounder.

She kicked the horse hard in the flank. She didn't care

where he ran. She just wanted to get away. But Mastiff read her thoughts. As the horse leaped into motion, he reached out an arm as thick as an oak trunk and pulled Rounder up short. Keeping a tight hold on the rein, he kicked his own horse. "Come on, Al. Let's go. We'll ditch the kid in the forest."

The horse thieves set off at a canter, traveling due north, and Hannah followed helplessly behind. Ditch the kid? Would they leave her there lost, alone and on foot, to try to find her way out as best she could? Or would they want to make sure she could never identify them?

She gulped. She hadn't even packed a pocket knife to defend herself with.

Hannah's head whirled with ideas. Perhaps she could fling herself off Rounder before the men had a chance to carry out their intentions. But the frozen ground whipped by at an alarming pace. And the road was passing between more wetlands with nowhere to run to. Besides all that, if she lost Rounder, she'd have no home to return to anyway. So she buried her hands in the horse's mane and clung to him, her panic growing with every step.

A half mile farther on, the road climbed slightly. The swamp fell away, replaced by thick undergrowth. To her left, the trees cleared, revealing a sizeable lake. And suddenly, seemingly right in her ear, something screamed.

It was a wild, piercing sound that dwindled to a snarl. Mastiff's horse bolted, and Rounder threw his head high, snapping one of the frozen reins. With a shriek of panic, he twisted in the air and catapulted Hannah into the trees at the side of the road. The trailing rein slashed her across the face.

And then she knew nothing.

***

At first Hannah heard only the drum. *Boom! Boom!*

145

Boom! It pounded with maddening regularity, filling the air, filling her body till her head ached with the noise. Then she realized there was no noise, only the pounding, the aching, the throbbing coming from just over her right ear. With a moan, she opened her eyes.

She lay in a dark room. Firelight flickered on the low, blackened beams above her. A cool wetness touched her forehead.

"You had quite a spill, Little Miss." A bass voice floated out of the darkness, smooth and earthy like the deep lowing of cattle.

"Where am I?" she asked, gasping at the pain it caused her.

"You's in the home of Ezra Jones." A blurry face leaned into her line of vision. Hannah was aware of very white teeth. "And I be Ezra Jones."

She tried to sit up, but a heavy hand thwarted her efforts. "Don't be hastenin', Little Miss. Jus' lie back and let yo' thoughts settle up."

She collapsed onto the bed out of sheer weariness.

"Dat's better. Missus Jones be makin' you some broth to get yo' strength back."

Hannah closed her eyes, trying to remember how she came to be here. She knew she had been cold. Very cold. Her fingertips still tingled with hot, new blood. She'd been frightened. And alone. No, she hadn't been alone; she'd been with Rounder.

"Rounder!" She sprang upright, memories overwhelming her. "Where's Rounder? Where's my horse?"

The soothing voice rolled over her again. "Yo' horse be jus' fine. He in da stable out back."

"But, but he ran away! There was a scream! A horrible scream. What—?" She started to tremble.

"Dat be a terrible big cat, Little Miss. I hear 'em, too. He run away when I shoot my gun. And den I find yo'

146

horse caught by one rein and you sleepin' peaceful-like beside him."

Now Hannah could see Ezra Jones clearly. He was a large black man, with broad shoulders and a round, smiling face. A fluff of gray hair added grace to his humble appearance. Hannah stared at the strange face, darker than any she had ever imagined.

Ezra reached behind her and fluffed up a feather pillow. "Here come Missus Jones. Sit back and eat up what she feed you, now."

Hannah's eyes had adjusted to the gloom, and she studied the woman who approached her holding a wooden bowl. Like her husband, she had rich, dark skin, full lips, and grizzled hair. She also had a thick figure that might have been the cause of her heavy limp.

"You do like Ezra say." The woman spoke brusquely, lacking the warm tones of her husband. But her hand was gentle as she spooned the rich liquid into Hannah's mouth.

As she ate, Hannah glanced around the tiny house. It was a cabin made of logs, like the one her parents had lived in. A fireplace had been cut out of one wall and a chimney built around it and daubed with mud. On one side of the blaze stood a table and two stools; on the other side was a handcrafted rocking chair. The small bedstead she lay in took up most of the opposite wall. She could see a ladder leading to a hole in the ceiling. At its base stood a wooden box filled with tools. That was all.

Mrs. Jones scraped the bottom of the bowl. The broth in Hannah's belly radiated warmth, and she could feel her eyes pulling closed.

"Res' yo'self, now, Little Miss," Ezra told her.

She fought to stay awake. "But you've nowhere to sleep," she argued.

"Don't you worry 'bout us, now," he rumbled with that gentle smile. "We's made do without a bed afore now."

147

Hannah had no energy to argue. The soft feathers, the warm soup, the crackle of flames all contributed to send her into a deep, untroubled sleep.

***

Hannah awoke to the smell of frying salt pork. The cabin was still dim, the only light coming from a single paper-covered window. Mrs. Jones was bent over the hearth, her wide back turned, but Hannah saw no sign of Ezra.

She sat up carefully. Her head still ached, but the torturous pounding of last night had subsided. At the sound, the black woman glanced over her shoulder. "Breakfas' be done directly," she said.

Hannah swung her legs over the side of the bed and stood up. The room toppled, but she forced herself to walk to the fire. If she hoped to reach Allegan, she must make her body obey. "Can I help with anything?" she offered.

"I been makin' breakfas' in dis cabin my own self for years. You set." She indicated the rocking chair. "Don' need to patch up no split heads dis mornin'."

The woman wasn't unkind, but Hannah had the distinct impression that her presence was unwanted. She sat without argument.

A few minutes later, as Mrs. Jones set the board, Ezra came through the door stamping snow from his boots. Hannah caught a glimpse of white yard, gray sky, and dark trees before the man's frame filled the doorway. He was difficult to see against the sudden glare of light, but when he closed the door she could make out his teeth in the shadows.

"Little Miss outta bed. Dis be good." He hung his coat and muffler on a peg pounded between the logs of the wall then crossed to the fire—it took only three strides—and held his hands out to the blaze. "Yo' horse be keepin' ol' Jack

148

company out in da stable, no worse for his fright. He hab his breakfast a'ready."

"Thank you, Mr. Jones."

"Been plain ol' Ezra mos' of my life. How you feeling, Little Miss?"

"You can call me Hannah—" she told him, but as the glow of the fire fell fully on the man, she uttered a gasp. The left side of his face and neck were crisscrossed with pink scars.

"What happened to you?"

He traced one of the welts with a thick forefinger. "Dis be da mark of a horsewhip."

"Someone did that to you with a riding crop?" she asked, incredulous.

He grunted and turned back to the fire without further comment.

Mrs. Jones called them to the table. Ezra indicated one of the two chairs. "You takes da stool, Little Miss, an' I'll set in da rocker. You'll never reach da vittles in dat big ol' chair." When they were all seated, he bowed his head and prayed in his deep voice, "Thank you, Lord, fo' enough food to fill our bellies again dis day. Amen."

Hannah's injury didn't seem to affect her appetite, and the simple meal tasted wonderful. Eggs, crisply fried pork, bread toasted over the fire, and a white porridge she had never seen before that Ezra called "grits." To wash it down, a glass of buttermilk sat beside each place, along with a hot, nutty drink that reminded her of coffee.

Ezra took a long pull at his buttermilk and turned to her with a frank question. "So where a youngster like you be going all by herself las' night, Miss Hannah?"

"I was on my way to Allegan to sell my horse." The memory of the two drunken men came back to her, and she told the Joneses the story of her abduction.

Ezra frowned. "Hm, reckon dat cat come along at jus'

da right moment. I wonder 'bout dose two fellas." He drifted off into silence again.

After several bites, Hannah ventured, "I still need to get to Allegan, but I'm afraid I'm out of my reckoning. Do you think you could tell me the way?"

"Sure. Go back half a mile and take da firs' road wes'. But why you sellin' yo' horse? Seems like a right fine animal to be partin' with."

Hannah's face fell. She wasn't at all certain she was doing the right thing. "I have to sell him, Ezra. My pa's away fighting, and if I don't get the money to repay a loan, my family will lose our farm."

Ezra sat back in the rocker and rubbed the gray stubble on his chin. "Family always come firs'." He stretched out his long legs.

Hannah glanced again at the scars on the man's face. "Ezra," she asked tentatively, "were you a slave? Did your owner do that to you?"

Mrs. Jones made a guttural sound. Her face was tense and proud, and Hannah knew she had spoken out of turn.

Ezra glanced up at his wife. "She ask innocent, Sarah. How a chil' from dese parts understan' otherwise?"

"I'm sorry," Hannah apologized. "I shouldn't pry."

"S'all right, Little Miss. If dare be hope of change, young'uns need truth. 'Sides, you should understan' what yo' daddy sacrificin' fo'."

Ezra heaved a great sigh that lifted his ribcage and set it down again. "I use to belong to a man named Jeremiah Barker, meanest cuss in all o' Georgia. His wife be jus' as bad. She da one give me dese marks. But her husban' done worse.

"Weren't always so bad. I live many years with a good man named Peters. Didn't care fo' being no one's slave, but I's never tempted to run off under Marse Peters. Life weren't so bad to risk hounds or da hangman's noose. Den

150

some of my family sold off here, some there, and my sister Julia and I's drug off to Old Man Barker." His face darkened. "And time come when dogs and noose soun' better'n livin'.

"Seven years I work ever' day. Never a Sabbath res' or a Christmas holiday. Whip if I's too slow. Chains if I looks sulky. Fists, nails, clubs, whatever da white man take a fancy to. Marse only had four slaves, so we all feel da lash too of'en.

"I met my Sarah an' need Marse Barker's permission to marry, but he won't give it. We jump over da broom anyway an' has five beautiful children: two girls and three boys. Don' know where none of 'em is. All sold off."

He looked out the window with raw pain in his eyes, even after so many years. Mrs. Jones stood quickly and began clearing the table.

"Did you run away?" Hannah asked softly.

He didn't answer, and Hannah knew the question was foolish. Of course he had, and suddenly the Emancipation Proclamation took on enormous significance. "No one can take you back," she told him. "President Lincoln made a law that forbids the return of runaways after the turn of the year. That's only one more week. I studied it in school."

He nodded. "We heard rumors. Can't read, and we keep most to our ownselves, but we heard tell o' such a law. It a good one."

"How did you end up in Allegan County?" she asked.

"Went to Detroit firs'. Lef' word for my sister if she follow, but dey's slavers all over dat city. So we settled where dare ain't so many people and had us one more son. He all growed up now. Moved away. Comes to visit every now an' den, but I ain't seen my sister evermore."

Ezra was silent for a long time, and Hannah could hear the slosh of a butter churn behind her. She felt such pity for the old couple. In her sheltered corner of Michigan, she had

151

no idea such suffering existed. Her own hardships paled by comparison.

She tried to decide if Ezra's story, and all the others like it, made the war with the South worth the cost, but she couldn't answer that. Surely there must have been a better way. But she did feel a new pride in her father, and in her brother, and in Michigan and the North. A pride, not for the bloody heroics of a battlefield, but for noble ideals and for setting to rights of a very old wrong.

"Thank you, Ezra, for your help."

He waved her away and his grin came back. "Think nothin' of it, Little Miss."

She wanted to linger in the cozy little cabin and share the warm understanding she'd found that spanned age and race, but she had to get to Allegan. She stood up. "I don't live very far away. Perhaps I could visit again sometime?"

"I'd like dat," Ezra agreed.

He pulled on his coat and muffler and soon delivered Rounder to her saddled and bridled. The horse was, indeed, in fine condition, and before she rode out of the yard she thanked the old man again.

"Miss Hannah, when you sees yo' father again, you thank him fo' me."

Chapter Sixteen

Hannah rode up Monroe Street looking for some clue that would direct her to the horse dealer, Mr. Rochester. The town was much bigger than Wayland, with a row of houses overlooking the river and cross streets crammed with storefronts. Some were decorated with greenery and twined about with ribbons, all gussied up like Christmas merrymakers. Others glowered out at her with stony blankness, unfamiliar and uninviting.

The streets of town swarmed with people, more than Hannah had ever seen in one place. They walked. They rode on horseback. They traveled in small cutters, large sledges, farm wagons modified with runners, and even one low lumber sleigh. Under so many hooves, the snow had churned into gritty muck that scabbed over with the last hard freeze.

She turned down Chestnut Street, which speared the center of town, and gaped up at the solid row of buildings stretching three stories into the air. It didn't take long to pass through to another loop of the river, with its docks and warehouses, mill and lumberyard, and a huge wooden bridge that spanned the water.

No one on the busy street offered to help or even glanced at Hannah. Though she thrilled with the excitement of returning to the city, now that she was here, a small part of her regretted that she had no one to share it with.

Rounder suddenly nickered and bobbed his head. As if conjured up by her vague disappointment, a call rang out from across the street.

"Hannah!"

It was Joel!

She jumped down and waved, tugging Rounder toward him.

Her brother dodged around a team and grabbed her in a bear hug. "Fool girl! Don't you know you could have been hurt or lost or killed? Thunderation, I'm relieved to see you're okay! I never thought you'd actually set off on one of those crazy schemes you're always dreaming up."

"Oh, don't be a grandma," she scorned, pushing away. "I'm fine."

Joel shook her gently. "I don't know what's gotten into you lately. Fighting with Justin like the devil and now running off. I'd like to take you over my knee and tan your hide. Mama's worried sick about you."

"I had to come, Joel," she insisted.

"If I hadn't run into Mr. Stockton, I never would have known where to look. And good thing Rounder recognized me, or I'd have passed you by."

She grew more adamant. "I told you, I had to come!"

"You didn't have to do anything but stay home and behave yourself for a change."

"Don't you see it, Joel?" she pleaded. "I couldn't save the wheat, I couldn't earn enough money to pay the loan, and I couldn't be the son Pa wanted, but I darn well will not fail him in this. I will not lose our farm!" Tears she had kept penned up for months bit at her eyes, threatening to break loose.

154

Joel looked stunned, like she'd hit him over the head with a sawmill slab. "What did you say?"

"I said I can't let Pa down again, Joel."

"No, about being a son—"

"Pa wanted another one so badly." She sniffed, refusing to open the floodgates. "I tried, Joel. I tried to take Jeremy's place, but I can't do it anymore. I have to be me, whatever that is. I hope Pa won't be too disappointed."

Joel listened, his eyes wide and incredulous. Then slow understanding filled them. He groaned and rubbed both hands over his face and into his hair, setting it on end. "Hannah, what do you remember of Jeremy?"

She focused on Rounder, patting his soft muzzle. "Not much. I remember going to Mrs. Patton's house with you and Maddy and Seth. When we came home we had to be real quiet. And I remember Doctor Graves coming and going a lot.

"But mostly I remember Pa crying and crying, walking around the house cradling that blanket in his arms. And for the first time, I couldn't reach him, Joel. He was in that room, but he was somewhere far away. I guess that day I realized his world was made up of more than just me."

She wrapped her arms around herself. "Funny, I don't remember Mama at all. I just remember that for days Pa wasn't my Pa, and it scared me. I guess I've never forgotten how much he loved that baby."

"Hannah," Joel spoke gravely, "there was another baby he loved just as much as that one. I was only three then, but I remember Pa cradling it, talking to it, kissing it, showing it off to anyone who would stop to look inside the blanket."

Hannah looked up blankly.

"You, goose!" he exclaimed. "Pa loves you more than anything! And he loves you because you're Hannah Grace Wallace, not because you have tried for years to be Jeremy

Tyler Wallace."

She turned away, but Joel grabbed her shoulders and forced her to listen. "If you had been born anyone else, who would have drawn Pa pictures of squirrels and woodchucks? Who would have told him those silly fairy tales? Who would have accompanied him on every trip to town or listened so attentively when he told stories at night? Who would have been Hannah?

"You don't need to do anything special for Pa to be proud of you. You're already special to him. And if we lost the farm, he would love you just as much."

Her brother's words were like honey on a sore throat. Like scratching an itch she couldn't reach. She had so needed to hear them, especially now, when all she had left was herself. And whatever that was, she finally allowed herself to believe it might be enough.

"Do you think Pa will be angry?"

"That you ran off? Probably."

"No. I mean angry that I'm going to sell Rounder."

"I would have done it myself if I'd needed to, and Pa would have been very sorry to lose him. But we are his family, and the farm is our home. What in the world is more important to him than that?"

She cocked an eyebrow at him. "You said if you needed to."

A slow grin creased his face. "That's right. Because we don't."

Hannah sucked in her breath. "You mean—?" She hardly dared hope.

"That's what I was trying to tell everybody yesterday when you ran off half-cocked. We have the money to pay off the loan."

Hannah's mouth dropped open. "How?"

Joel laughed out loud. "When I asked Mrs. Patton to buy our north pasture, she turned me down. She knew how

156

we felt about losing that land. Instead, she suggested a lease. We've been waiting for word from Mr. Patton. I never mentioned it in case it didn't work out, but she got a reply from him two days ago. He's returning next month with new stock to improve his herd, and he agreed wholeheartedly. So Mrs. Patton signed a five-year lease and paid the money up front. Mama sewed it into my pant leg. We just have to visit the post office."

***

It didn't take long to arrange a money order. They left the post office with a receipt in hand and a lighter step. The farm was secure.

As they passed the land office, Joel pulled away. "I want to step in here a moment. I have a hunch."

The building was a plain board square, drafty, and heated with an iron stove. A middle-aged man sat behind an untidy desk. "Can I help you?"

Joel stepped up. "Yes, I'd like some information on land fraud, please."

"Going into business for yourself, son?" the man asked with a wry grin.

Joel grimaced. "No sir."

"Well, I don't see too much of it hereabouts. Used to. But Michigan is filling up like a bucket left outside on a rainy day, and most crooks find these parts too much bother for too little profit. But out west where there is so much unclaimed land, or up in the northern forests, now that's another story. What with million-acre railroad grants and the new homesteading law, seems like someone comes up with another scam every day."

Joel thought about that a moment. "Have you ever heard of Mercurial Landholdings?"

The man raised one eyebrow. "As a matter of fact, that

name came to my attention very recently. Heard some complaints from homesteaders out near where the Grand Rapids and Indiana rail line is supposed to go through. Why? You have a run-in with them?"

"You could say that." Joel explained what happened.

He gave them a sympathetic smile. "Same story I've heard. Lawson's a small-timer, a con man, really. Not much I can do except put out a warning."

"I figured as much." Joel looked at Hannah, who just wanted to put the whole thing behind them.

"Let's go home, Joel."

Outside, Joel pulled a few coins from his pocket. "I have a little money left over. How about lunch at the Allegan House and a ride home on the stage? I'll ride Rounder."

His words matched Hannah's thoughts exactly, and nothing had ever sounded so good.

Chapter Seventeen

The house smelled of popped corn and the little ever-green tree standing in the front window. Christmas had come and gone a week ago, but Justin had insisted on cutting and dragging the tree home that morning—by himself.

Doctor Graves had finally given the okay, and Maddy and Justin flooded back into the quiet house, filling it with energy, arguments, and laughter. Hannah hadn't realized how people brought life to the rooms until she lived and worked in them alone. They gathered now around the tree, draping it with homemade garlands while Mama sat watching from her rocking chair, hardly coughing at all.

Hannah was filled with a contentment the late holiday couldn't fully account for. The end of the year had passed, 1863 had begun, and she couldn't know what it would bring. Her father and brother were still away fighting, and the war hung uncertainty over the whole nation. But her family had strength and resilience in their blood. They were tucked snugly in the house they had built, on land they still owned, and there was nowhere else on earth Hannah wanted to be.

"Mama?" Justin broke into her thoughts. "Will God be mad that we're not celebrating on his birthday?"

Mama's eyes sparkled, but before she could answer they heard stomping on the step outside the door.

Mama's face suddenly paled. "That sounds like—"

"Pa!" they all yelled as the door pushed open.

He looked thin and haggard, but he was home.

Uncertainty seized Hannah, holding her back as her siblings rushed him at the door. She rubbed her hands against her skirt. Would Pa truly want to see her?

Pa grabbed each of his children up in a bear hug. Then he turned to Mama, holding out an envelope. "My discharge papers."

Mama's tears fell then. "Glory be!" And she stumbled into his embrace.

After a moment, Pa pulled away and glanced around. "Where's Hannah?"

She stepped forward shyly. "Here, Pa."

"Well, what are you waiting for, girl?"

Her hesitancy dropped away, and she threw herself in her father's arms. He hugged her tightly, and the tears she had bound so carefully broke free and galloped down her cheeks. "I missed you, Peanut."

Her face pressed against the rough fabric of his uniform. "I missed you too, Pa!"

He let her go and spread out his hands, encompassing the house and the barn and the fields. "You don't know how good it feels to come home!"

Hannah met Joel's eyes and they exchanged a secret smile. She did know. And she also knew that, war or no war, the Wallace family was going to weather 1863 just fine.

Author's Note

I have attempted to recreate the history of Wayland as accurately as possible. I've taken the liberty of using some actual names from old records, including the doctor, schoolteacher, shopkeepers, and tradesmen, though all personalities and descriptions are completely fictionalized. Most notable of these is Mr. Nelson Chambers, who was the first settler within the town limits. He built the Wayland House in 1855. The town was first known as Chamber's Corners, though I chose to call it by its modern name. Also, Mr. Norton Briggs was postmaster and toll collector for years. My apologies if these liberties have offended any descendants. Mr. Lawson, the Wallaces, Mr. Covington, and the Carvers are all fictional.

The Toll Road's arrival in 1854 spurred Wayland's growth. The town as I have described it is based on an 1861 plat map and embellished with guesswork. But it changed and grew so rapidly, with businesses relocating along the Plank Road, that it scarcely looks like the next map drawn only a few years later, which closely resembles the town of today.

The land conflict featured in this story never happened, although speculators often did precede the railroads. The Grand Rapids and Indiana line finally reached Wayland in 1870.

Fever and ague (*ague* means chills) was the most common complaint of homesteaders. Now known as malaria, it was spread by mosquitoes. These regular shakes and fever were a part of life for all settlers of America's frontiers until

161

swamplands were drained and the disease died out.

The Michigan 17th Infantry was one of the state's finest. I have accurately portrayed its formation and distinguished service. Company D did, in fact, include over thirty men from Wayland and surrounding townships, over 40 percent of whom were killed or wounded in the battles I have described.

The Civil War raged from April 12, 1861 until April 9, 1865. It left 620,000 men dead, a number that exceeds the combined deaths of all America's other wars, and created an untold number of widows and orphans. Countless others lived with diseases and injuries sustained during the war. The final outcome settled the issue of states' rights and put an end to the evil of slavery, but these tragic totals leave me questioning how a nation as great as ours had to resort to fighting. Like Hannah and Mr. Carver and Mr. Covington, I wonder if there could have been a better way.

The Close of a
Long Family History

1864

Jefferson Jones (son of Ezra Jones and cousin to Malachi Watson)
features in book three of the Divided Decade
Trilogy, Beneath the Slashings.

"Jefferson, did you hear Governor Blair is raising up a Colored regiment downstate?"

My partner, a hard-living Irishman from Pittsburg, and I alternated swings on a giant white pine. My heart thrummed at his words. "You're sure of that, O'Malley?"

"Heard it from Mac. His last food shipment was packed in old newspapers. They're calling it the First Michigan Colored."

Ever since Emancipation, the war had become my own. Reason would say that a man whose family tree had been bludgeoned by slavery would make an ideal soldier, but time and again Colored volunteers had been turned away by the government. O'Malley's news lit a fire in my blood. I knew the risk—the glamor of war had long since blown away like powder smoke, but the principal behind it remained. I burned to see the task of freedom carried out.

O'Malley grinned, his teeth stained by his passion for

163

smoking tobacco. "Guess enough white men finally died for Uncle Sam to take you fellows seriously. You joining up?"

"Reckon so."

"The boss man won't be happy. Can't make quota with everyone off soldering."

"Does Mac have any more details?"

O'Malley shrugged. "Go get the article from him before he uses it to cook biscuits."

A few days before Christmas, I collected my pay and headed for home. My parents lived in a snug little shack near Allegan. I hitched a ride as far as Grand Rapids, but it took me two days to walk the last forty-five miles. I swung open the barn door sometime before midnight Christmas Eve.

Lantern light awoke me the next morning. "Jefferson?" Pa gasped. "What are you doin' here? You ill?"

"Morning, Pa." I grinned ruefully, fighting off the effects of sleep. "I was going to surprise you."

"You did." He chuckled, the sound low and rumbling like the shifting of rock. "You sho'ly did." But his laughter had an undercurrent of concern. A lumberjack never left camp until the spring thaw. "Let me feed ol' Jack den we'll spring you on yo' mama."

I don't know how a heart can feel as soft and warm as a feather pillow and as heavy as lead shot all at the same time, but that's just how I felt walking in my parent's door that morning. "Merry Christmas, Mama."

She nearly dropped the plate of cornbread she was carrying. "Lan' sakes, child! Let me look at you!" I was in her arms one breath later.

That was a fine day. The snow fell outside in big white flakes while we sipped Pa's hot cider before the fire. Mama whipped up mashed potatoes, dried apple pie, and a home-cured ham that left me feeling a mite sorry for the fellas left in camp. Even the Christmas story got read proper that year,

164

seeing I was the only one who could read. It was the kind of holiday that stacks up against even the best of memories. But I couldn't put off my news forever.

"Mama, Pa." A look of expectation crossed their faces. I think they already knew. "I've decided to take my place in the Union army."

Pa slapped a hand on my thigh. "I'm right proud of you, son. If I was ten years younger, I'd be signin' my name right next to yo's."

I figured Pa would react that way. He'd always been as steady as an old plow horse. But I was unprepared for Mama's response. Her face grew grave. "Be careful, Jefferson. You goin' to a dark land."

"I know, Mama. You and Pa have told me stories."

"You can't know 'less you been dare. You gunna see things that break yo' heart."

I'd never known slavery. I'd been a passenger in my mama's belly when she and Pa fled north. "I'll do everything I can to change that."

She grinned then. "I'm gunna worry 'bout you every day, but I'd be sore pleased if you chose otherwise."

I smiled back at her. "I have a few weeks before we rendezvous in Detroit."

At the mention of that city, Pa and Mama shared a glance that changed the atmosphere of the room. Pa cleared his throat. "Will you be lookin' when you get there?"

"Course I will, Pa."

He nodded, his eyes gone off somewhere far away. "Maybe this time."

Mama touched his arm. "Don' get yo' hopes up too high, Ezra. Maybe she didn't come."

"She came," he countered. "Julia—she came."

It ate Pa up something awful knowing that he'd had to leave his sister behind in Georgia all those years ago. They planned to meet in Detroit, but Pa had never been able to

165

find her. He'd been waiting more than twenty years.

"I'll turn over every stone, Pa. I promise."

"I know you will, son." He leaned back heavily in his chair, massaging the ache in one knee. "Jefferson, I've a mind to hear the Exodus story if you's willing." And so we celebrated both Christmas and Passover that afternoon.

The days flew by. The routine I'd grown up with was an easy one to fall back into. Milking the cow, chopping firewood, feeding the chickens, lifting some of the burden off my parents' aging shoulders. It was light work compared to the woods, and it ended much too quickly.

When it came time to say good-bye, Mama found her tears. Pa stood stoically at her side, one arm around her shoulders. I couldn't help thinking how weary they looked, how fragile. I had plenty of time to regret our parting on the long walk to Kalamazoo. In that city, I spend the little money I had kept for myself to buy railway passage. I slept most of the way to Detroit.

The city's sheer size amazed me, with its endless skyline and crowded streets. There were so many people! How did I even begin to look for one woman? It was like searching for a coin on the Lake Huron shoreline. I stood before the railway station in a haze of bewilderment, much preferring the toil and dangers of a lumber camp.

I caught the eye of a pleasant-faced man with a mop of brown curls. He sat in the front of a bob sleigh marked "River Street Inn," obviously waiting for patrons. "Excuse me, sir," I hailed. "Can you tell me the way to the nearest Colored congregation?"

"I'll do one better. Climb in and I'll drop you off. It's hardly out of my way."

"Bless you, sir," I replied and climbed into the seat beside him. Twenty minutes later I alighted at the door of St. Matthew's Episcopal Church. Waving to the hotel man, I entered the church with hope leaping like frogs in my belly.

An elderly janitor answered my question with a regretful shake of his head. "I'm sorry, son. There is no Julia Watson in attendance at St. Matthews. You can try the Methodists."

He gave me detailed directions but with all my detours and wrong turns, finding the church took the better part of an hour. Locating someone to whom I could pose my question took considerably longer. Two hours passed before a choir director opened the church for an evening practice. By then my stomach was rumbling and my hands and feet had grown painfully cold.

Unfortunately, the director didn't know my aunt either. I bowed under the weight of my disappointment. "Are there any other congregations I can try?"

The fellow smiled sympathetically. "There's still the Baptists. You're in luck. Mrs. Johnson will be along in a few minutes. She was a regular member until last winter when she moved in with her son and joined our congregation. If your aunt attended Second Baptist in the last twenty-six years, Mrs. Johnson will know."

I fidgeted like a child awaiting the close of a school day.

Mrs. Johnson was a diminutive woman with the presence of a field commander. Her glare most certainly kept Methodist children on the straight and narrow. "Julia Watson? Of course I know Julia Watson. Fine, strong Christian woman. Raised up a son all by herself. What business do you have with her?"

My heart began a joyous racing. "She's my aunt."

The woman's face split into a mask of happy wrinkles. "Her brother Ezra's child?"

"Yes!"

"Brother Danford, go stop my son! He's got to drive this child across town!"

Moments later I was settled in a small cutter. Mrs.

167

Johnson had given her son very emphatic directions, and we moved through the snow at a good clip. My pulse kept time with the horses' hooves. What was my aunt like? Why had she raised her son alone? Would I meet him, too? I wished my father could have been there with me.

We pulled up before a two-story structure with a sign in the front yard that read "River Street Inn." I glanced at it a second time. "You're sure this is the place?" I asked the driver.

"Shore is. Mrs. Watson runs the kitchen for Mr. Milford."

A black woman appeared on the hotel's front porch just then and began sweeping snow from the walk. The driver nudged me and smiled. "Go on."

I approached the woman cautiously. "Julia Watson?"

She turned around. "Yes?" Then her eyes got huge and her hands flew to her mouth. "Ezra!"

I shook my head. "I'm his son, Jefferson."

The broom clattered to the ground. With her embrace, my family closed the cover on a long family mystery.

Divided Decade Trilogy
Book Three

Manistee River Valley, Michigan Wilderness, 1865

After four uncertain years of war, Grace Nickerson is desperate to return to a sense of normalcy. But soon after her father returns, he sells the farm and drags the family off to a lumber camp in Michigan's northern wilderness. Then a series of accidents within the camp proves intentional. Who is sabotaging the camp, and why? Will the winter in the woods bring the healing Grace needs? Or will it drive a wedge into her family?

Beneath the Slashings carries the series to the Michigan wilderness, in which many returning veterans made a new start, and concludes the story of the Jones and Watson families.

Find free downloadable lesson plans
and additional titles by Michelle Isenhoff at
www.michelleisenhoff.com.

Sign up for Michelle's new release email list
on her website.

Made in the USA
Lexington, KY
05 April 2015